# ASHOKA'S SECRET

# ASHOKA'S SECRET

Chinmay Patgaonkar

NU VOICE
PRESS

First published by NU VOICE PRESS 2024
An imprint of Hubhawks Pvt. Ltd
www.nuvoicepress.com



This is a work of fiction and all characters and incidents described in this book are the product of the author's imagination. Any resemblance to actual persons, living or dead, is entirely coincidental.



ISBN: 978-81-966888-1-3

Typeset by Saanvi Graphics, Noida
Printed at Thomson Press
Published by Nu Voice Press

*Buddham sharanam gacchami*
*Sangam sharanam gacchami*
*Dhammam sharanam gacchami*

I take refuge in the Buddha
I take refuge in the Sangha
I take refuge in the Dharma

# ACKNOWLEDGMENTS

My sister, Janhavi: I look up to her for her love of history, particularly ancient Indian. I pursued studying history and started loving the subject by seeing you talk about it continuously during the dinner table conversations for as long as I can remember. The main character is based on you—the main character's passion for history accurately resembles your love for the subject of ancient India. You are my real-life Robert Langdon, and the inspiration for my constant curiosity about history. Thank you!

My history teachers, Mr. Jayakrishnan Nair, Ms. Shalaka, and Ms. Dhanashree, who nurtured my profound interest in history and taught it as an interesting story with perspectives rather than just a collection of facts. I reminisce about our engaging discussions about history, and I would like to thank your patience and persistence in dealing with my constant mischievous antics.

My childhood friend, Vallari, with whom I share a love for books, the craziest inside jokes, and multiple references of movies and shows. She has supported me throughout this book's journey with her presence and suggestions. It is she who taught me resilience.

A big thank you to NuVoice Press and Hubhawks for making this book come to life. I would like to thank you from the bottom of my heart for making this book happen and for guiding me through each part of the process. To Kevin, Abhishek, Abhijeet, Tripti, Vini, Vedika, Navya, Tanvi, Deepika, Naghma, Kiran, Abhinav and a few names that I have missed out on, I am truly grateful for your guidance and for believing in me and this story. All the calls and the discussions about the story, the characters, the marketing, and the publishing have made this journey quite memorable. You guys are the best! Thank you so much!

This book is dedicated to Advay, my cousin who left our family on 11th March 2023. This book is a gift for all your smiles you splashed at us that shunned our tears and worries about you. In fond remembrance of my dear departed cousin who taught us the power of smile—lots of love to you my baby brother—this is a gift to you

–From Chinu dada

# DISCLAIMER

This book is a complete work of fiction. Events, people, timelines associated in this story are all coincidental and a part of the author's imagination. The author has no intent of offending, criticising, or slandering any person, race, religion, caste, community, institution, or any ideology. Considering that the book is a fictional narrative based on historical events, the author recommends that this book is not to be taken as a serious source of studying history. Nowhere in this novel does the author confirm the existence of any secret society whatsoever. This book is supposed to be enjoyed as a fictional, historical-thriller and to be taken with a pinch of salt. Again, before you read this book, let the author remind you once again: It is a complete work of fiction. Happy reading!

*"History is a pack of lies about events that never happened told by people who were never there."*

*—George Santayana*

# Part One

# CHAPTER 1

**261 BCE**
**Kalinga**
**Bharat**

The Mauryan empire had declared a war against the Kalingan empire, leading to a huge bloodbath. Kalinga was a kingdom, spread somewhere from south-eastern Andhra Pradesh to Odisha around 261 BCE. A time when India or what then was called Bharat, was a wealthy country—rich in science, spirituality, knowledge, and power. The war of Kalinga had just been fought, and the dead bodies lay down on the ground with blood oozing out of them. Hundreds of soldiers battled against the strong and the powerful Mauryan army whose king was Ashoka, the heir of the Mauryan empire.

Ashoka was standing in the midst of an empty ground piled up with dead bodies; some rolling over the foothills, like sacks of potatoes, towards the river. The rich green grass of the ground had suddenly turned red with blood. Ashoka was speechless, tears falling from his eyes just like the blood of the innocent Kalingans. Ashoka wanted an *Akhand* Bharat—an undivided Bharat ruled by the Mauryan empire—a dream he inherited from his grandfather Chandragupta Maurya. Chandragupta took reins of the country when Alexander's hordes were touching India and Bharat was in disarray. It was Chandragupta who ruled Bharat and the master strategist Chanakya who created a strong and powerful empire with Chandragupta as the king. If Kalinga was captured then that meant that Ashoka had conquered the whole of Bharat, it would make Ashoka the greatest Mauryan King ever. His only aim turned out to be his greatest regret ever.

And here was Ashoka who wanted to maintain an Akhand Bharat, he wanted an undivided nation but to what extent could he go for it? His utopia of an undivided nation had painted the scenery of a horrific dystopian destruction at Kalinga. He wanted a unified empire and this is what he got. He was in the midst of a sea of dead bodies on the foothills of Kalinga. Innocent men, women, and children had fought bravely to not be subdued by the Mauryan empire. The Mauryans who were driven by their ambition to control the trade routes with south-east Asia. Chandragupta Maurya and Bindusara, his predecessors fought for that land. Ashoka was the only one who conquered Kalinga, he was a hero in the eyes of his well-wishers, his subjects, his ministers, his family, and his people. They saw him as a hero but it was

Ashoka who saw himself as a villain, a ruthless murderer who committed a massacre just for controlling trade.

Ashoka screamed, "Oh mercy to those murdered by me! I have failed my father and my grandfather. I may have continued my family's legacy; I may be a hero to my people but I have also been a murderer. A criminal. I am carrying the blood of innocent people. I have made the soil bloody. I wanted Kalinga so that the empire dominates overseas trade. I wanted to take over Kalinga to make my dead father and my dead grandfather proud! I want Akhand Bharat but not with blood and violence anymore. Where has humanity gone? Is this how humanity meets its downfall? Is this what Kaliyuga is? Is this how human nature will be? People hungry, brutal, and ruthless for power? For money?"

He was standing on the foothills of Kalinga facing the banks of the nearby Daya river. As he walked down towards the river, he saw an endless array of dead bodies. He kept questioning everything he had done so far. From killing his brothers for the ascension of the throne to the tyrannical hell that he had created to conquer more kingdoms. Once he had the majority of Bharat in his hands, his job to conquer Kalinga—a constitutional monarchy left undefeated from the Mauryan empire— was made easier.

Tears streamed from Ashoka's eyes like a waterfall. He looked around, and he saw an endless horizon of dead bodies, of blood, of dead horses, of swords, spears, and arrows pierced into multiple bodies and blood running from their bodies. He walked towards the banks of Daya nearby. He wanted to spend some time alone and away from the corpses. He saw the river polluted with blood, it was red. It seemed like there was more water in blood than blood in water. Ashoka sighed under his breath, "Bloody river!". He saw more dead bodies than ever. Thousands of people killed! All for power, money, and trade. Ashoka wept and screamed. He went blank. Tears could not stop flooding from his eyes. He felt lifeless, he realised that he did not have much mercy left. He had become ruthless, brutal, and hungry for power. He wanted to do something. He wanted to revive humanity in the dark age of Kaliyuga. He wanted to prevent another brutal war and its effects after what he just saw.

Suddenly, he saw the clouds showering rain from above. The sky was also turning pinkish-orange. Ashoka's guilt made him think that the sky too was reflecting the blood of the war. He saw the water droplets falling on him and saw them as the tears of Mauryan and Kalingan soldiers/ citizens. Innocent men, women, children, and brave soldiers of Kalingan and Mauryan army were wailing from heaven is what he imagined. He cried and screamed out his guilt, "I AM SORRY!" He could not stop his emotions, his guilt, his anger. His heart broke into a million pieces. His scared and horrific imagination made him hear voices from the windy breeze calling him a murderer.

He looked back and he saw no one, he just saw the bodies bowing down to him. Ashoka stood up and saw no other soul standing. Thousands of bloodied bodies bowed down to him as they gave up their soul to him. He could see that the Kalingans sacrificed their soul to him so that his empire could become even more powerful than what it already was. Bharat was an extremely rich country; however, Ashoka thought that he could make Bharat and the Mauryan empire even more powerful. He was greedy and he did not realise his greed till he saw the aftereffects of his greed.

He could not stop crying, he felt so breathless while crying that he puked. He wasn't sick, it was his guilt that made him vomit. He saw the vomit mixing with the bloody river.

Those horrors of Kalinga, he will never forget.

# CHAPTER 2

**250 BCE**
**Sarnath**
**Bharat**

Ashoka was traumatised by the events of Kalinga. He was depressed, dejected—emotionally destroyed. He could not bear the guilt within him. The horrific images from Kalinga could not be forgotten easily. It became a part of him. He wanted to prevent another Kalinga. He had never touched a sword or any other weapon at his palace in Pataliputra, the capital of Bharat. The Mauryan empire was founded by King Chandragupta Maurya who was guided by the well-known strategist and Prime Minister Chanakya. Later on, Bindusara, the son of Chandragupta took the reins and eventually died in 273 BCE. Then came Ashoka who took the reins of the empire. The name Ashoka meant "without any sorrow" but after the bloodshed in Kalinga, he was filled with sorrow, regret, and guilt.

Ashoka had several sleepless nights for a long while. He was unable to focus on anything, not because of sleep but because of the horrific images from Kalinga. His ministers tried to convince him that the Kalinga feat was a huge success, but he saw himself as a murderer. He had been carrying the blood on his hands. When he retired to bed, he closed his eyes and saw the dead bodies at Kalinga haunting his dreams. Every time he saw that, he felt like those innocent dead souls wanted to remind him of his karma.

His body language was different now. From how he used to carry himself as the powerful king—with class, with an attitude, with confidence. His body language differed after the Kalinga war—his shoulders lowered down, his body was stiff, he started slouching. His eyes used to be bold as a flame, and now his eyes were as dead as a zombie. He looked dull, bored, and lifeless.

He was not a very good-looking man. His skin was tanned and multiple cuts on his face from the wars he fought made him look hideous. Considering that he was barely getting any sleep, his face now carried dark circles. He was also not eating properly. He loved eating meat; however, since the Kalinga war, he was not ready to even take in a nibble of food till his wives convinced him to. He had not even touched meat after the bloodbath at Kalinga. He ignored the daily meetings in the royal court, he was always in his chambers. His ministers convinced him to step out of his royal quarters; however, he was reluctant.

Ashoka had killed his brothers, including his elder brother Sushim, who was the crown prince of the Mauryan empire. Ashoka's greed and brutal nature made him the king of the Mauryan empire. His policy of conquering other lands made him crown the title of "Chakravartin Samrat": the king of all kings. His grandfather, Chandragupta Maurya, and his wife, Maharani Devi, were devout Buddhists. His wife's religious influence on Ashoka after the Kalinga war, led him to join the path of Buddhism. A ruthless king who was the absolute contrary of peace, soon turned out to be accepting of peace, love, and humanity and gave up war, weapons, and violence.

One day, he decided to learn more about the Buddhist philosophy and travelled all the way to Sarnath, a place people may call an ancient civilisation or a Buddhist society about 10 kilometres away from what was then called Kashi or Anandvan in present-day Varanasi, Uttar Pradesh. Ashoka's chariot arrived in Sarnath. He stepped down from his chariot looking at one of the stupas in front of him. He could hear the Buddhist chants. The monks had started chanting the famous Buddhist mantra which could reach Ashoka's ears from a distance. He followed the sound leading him inside a stupa.

*Buddham sharanam gacchami*
*Sangam sharanam gacchami*
*Dhamman sharanam gacchami*

He could hear the chanting repeatedly, his body felt a wave of goosebumps, and his mind was elevating. He really felt that clarity in his mind, pulling him out of all the mess in his mind and his life. He walked inside one of the stupas as he heard the chanting "Buddham sharanam gacchami. Sangam sharanam gacchami. Dhamman sharanam gacchami" from the meditating monks. Ashoka too sat down and started chanting the mantra. Mantras are usually chanted 108 times as each chant represents a journey from one's material self to its highest spiritual self. After the chanting was over, they all looked at this stranger who had walked inside their stupa and smiled at him. The fellow monks walked outside the stupa. Ashoka was nervous to stop them.. He waited till the old monk was alone, not wanting to interrupt his conversation with the fellow younger monks.

Ashoka saw the elderly monk who was the guru and the chief of the Buddhist community of Sarnath, walking downwards on a slope towards his residential quarters. The door had been kept open. Ashoka glanced from a distance and observed what the chief monk of Sarnath was doing from the beginning of the slope going downhill. He saw the monk lighting a few candles and then sitting on a mat on the floor, starting to chant the famous Buddhist mantra *Om Mani Padme Hum.* The monk repeated the chant of "Om Mani Padme Hum" and moved his finger to the next bead after every chant of the six syllabled mantra.

Ashoka was keen and ready to learn about Buddhism. He walked slowly down the slope of the monk Samudra, who is considered to be the reincarnation of the Indo-Tibetan saint Padmasambhava. He walked inside and sat on a mat. He looked around Samudra's residence. As Ashoka settled inside the residence, he saw two sculptures. The first one was on his left, a meditating Buddha with candles lit, releasing an aromatic scent of lotus which is a significant flower in Buddhism.

Behind the meditating Samudra repeatedly chanting "Om Mani Padme Hum" and switching to the next bead of the 108 *japamaala* (string of beads used for praying or chanting), Ashoka saw the sculpture of Padmasambhava also known as Guru Rinpoche. He knew about the famous tantric, mystic, and Buddhist guru whose statue of resting on a lotus was in front of him, facing Samudra's back. The Buddhist folktale narrates that Guru Rinpoche: the precious master, was found as a baby resting on a floating lotus on a lake. Ashoka had read enough about Buddhism from the stories told by his wife Devi, and from some manuscripts that he had read in Takshashila and Nalanda University's books, shelved in their libraries. Some people consider Padmasambhava to be the

Second Buddha because of him spreading Buddhist teachings to Tibet during his lifetime.

Ashoka sat in front of Samudra on the floor. He shut his eyes and chanted the six-syllable mantra "Om Mani Padme Hum" with Guru Samudra. Minutes later, Samudra and Ashoka slowly opened their eyes together. Samudra's eyes smiled as Ashoka bowed down and greeted Samudra. "O' Master, Help me."

"Yes, how can I help you? Ashoka?" asked Samudra.

Ashoka was shocked by how Samudra knew his name, "Master, how do you know my name?"

Samudra calmly explained, "My name is Samudra. I am the reincarnation of Padmasambhava, also known as Guru Rinpoche: the precious master. You are Ashoka, the Chakravartin Samrat. About a hundred years ago in your past life as Jaya living in Magadh, you offered soil as alms to the enlightened Buddha hallucinating that filth to be food.

Lord Buddha predicted that a hundred years after the Buddha attains *nirvana,* that same boy would be Chakravartin Samrat Ashok, who will follow the path of Buddhism."

Ashoka started asking his list of unanswered queries, "I have killed my own brothers. I have tortured people. I have become entirely greedy, ruthless, and sadistic. I wish there was a way to change my destiny; if only I did not wage that war at Kalinga."

Samudra corrected Ashoka, "Destiny is not an 'if I did' but a 'when I will'."

Ashoka pleaded, "I need Buddhist spirituality to change me Guru Rinpoche! Please help me!"

"Change comes from within. Spirituality does not change you, it is just a medium through which change happens. The way a baby transitions from an adolescent, and an adolescent transitions into an adult, that is how you, Ashoka, will change from *Chandashok* to *Dhammashok*—from Ashoka the cruel to Ashoka the pious."

"What should I do to become a Buddhist?" asked Ashoka.

"Remember three refuges: *Buddham...sharanam...gacchami, Sangham...sharanam...gacchami, Dhammam...sharanam... gacchami.*"

The monk answered, "This mantra is divided into 3 sentences: Buddham sharanam gacchami means I seek refuge in the Buddha and spreading knowledge. Sangham sharanam gacchanmi—use the knowledge you have to spread it across the community for the good, and Dhammam sharanam gacchami—use the knowledge as your *dharma*; your duty, your purpose."

Ashoka joined his hands and bowed at the reincarnation of Padmasambhava, he thanked Samudra and promised him, "Guru Rinpoche, O' reincarnation of Padmasambhava, I promise that I shall walk on the path of *Dhamma* and contribute towards knowledge and humanity in the age of Kaliyuga."

Samudra smiled and said, "When the student is ready to learn and obtain knowledge, the teacher appears instantly." Ashoka bowed down and closed his eyes. Through magical powers that Samudra was gifted with, he disappeared in a fraction of a second. Ashoka lifted his head up and saw that Samudra had disappeared. After searching the entire residence from one room to another, he looked at the sculpture of Padmasambhava resting on the lotus and smiled. As he walked outside, he met his spiritual teacher and his master of Buddhism: Upadatta, who was going to mentor him and teach him about Buddhism.

"Chakravartin Samrat Ashok, I am your spiritual teacher Upadatta. I am going to take you on a journey of Buddhism so that you unlock your inner Buddha, your inner *Bodhidharma*: your awakening towards enlightenment!"

He realised that Buddhism advocates for peace, humanity, and harmony. Ashoka converted to Buddhism as he felt remorse for his past deeds and officially gave up war. He dropped his sword and embraced peace, harmony, and humanity. Ashoka decided to expand Buddhist teachings across the entire *Bharatvarsh*, with the company of Upadatta as his mentor.

# CHAPTER 3

**Lomas Rishi Caves**
**Pataliputra**
**A few years after Ashoka's conversion**

A few months had passed since Ashoka converted to Buddhism. He advocated for Buddhism and built multiple monasteries and stupas. He expanded Buddhism across the country and even beyond the borders of Bharat under his rule. It was midnight, the full moon was shining white and bright. Nine Buddhist monks with their heads covered walked inside a man-made cave called the Lomas Rishi Cave built during Ashoka's reign. One of the men used fire on a big stick as a torch and hung it on a wall. The emperor, Ashoka the Great walked in. The nine men uncovered their heads and bowed down to their king. Ashoka greeted them back with a bow and began speaking: "You must be wondering why all of you are here. You may see me as a hero for annexing Kalinga; however, you have not seen the bloodshed that happened there. I have and I blame myself for it. To prevent another horrifying incident like Kalinga or worse than the Kalinga war, I have decided to establish a secret society. A society that helps humanity, that helps the world when the world is in a massive crisis. I would like to call this society: the Nine Unknown."

One man from the group raised his hand. He asked, "What do we have to do as a part of The Nine Unknown, Chakravartin Samrat?"

"Each one of you is an expert in your field. All you have to do is preserve, research, revise, and revive your knowledge in books that will benefit humanity whenever the world is in crisis. To stabilise matters during an era of destruction and preventing a possible dystopia is the purpose of why this secret society has been created. You are not to be revealing of your identities as part of The Nine Unknown, and you must do your job in utmost secrecy. One more thing to add on is that this society must have nine individuals. Not more than nine, or less than nine. Exact nine individuals who will study and research more into their respective fields and preserve their knowledge. And, when the world is at its worst, it is then that we reveal these studies to those who strive to save it. If our knowledge falls into wrong hands, then the world will end up in complete chaos."

An old man asked, "What happens in case we retire or die, Chakravartin Samrat Ashok?"

Ashoka answered, "The successor of the particular field you are in will carry out your research." He also added, "The nine unknown can be from any part of the world. But they must be nine scholars."

He read the room; he noticed that a question mark had popped up on each of their heads, enquiring the significance of the limit of nine scholars only. More people would only help more information being gathered in the bowl of knowledge. He addressed, "The reason nine scholars are supposed to be a part of this society is because the number 9 is significant in our mythology. For example: The *navgraha* in Hindu astrology, nine universal elements in our philosophy, we celebrate *navratri* in festivals for nine nights. And not to forget that there have been nine influential ministers as a part of the council in the King's Court. This is why nine is a significant number for our society."

Another young gentleman who was a part of the nine asked, "What are the areas of study?"

"The nine of you have to work in nine different fields which are: Propaganda, Physiology, Microbiology, Alchemy, Communication, Gravity, Cosmology, Light, and Sociology."

He continued, "When the time is right and the world is ready to accept change, this secret society will revise and update its studies. If in case the world is in crisis or this country goes through a major calamity that these manuscripts can solve, then these nine manuscripts shall be revealed to help the world stabilise from a derailing situation. Keep this society a big, hidden secret, and ensure it lands in the right hands for the betterment of humanity."

"The three laws of Buddha that we all must follow the *bhavachakra* or our endless cycle of rebirths. Buddham sharanam gacchami: I seek refuge in Buddha and spreading knowledge. Sangam sharanam gacchami: Use the knowledge you have to spread it across the community for the good. Dhammam sharanam gacchami: Use the knowledge as your *dharma*, your duty, your purpose," he concluded.

# CHAPTER 4

**232 BCE**
**Kumrahar**
**Pataliputra**
**Bharat**

The Mauryan Palace in Kumrahar, governed under King Ashoka, was awaiting a news, an unpleasant one. Their King, Ashoka the Great was on his deathbed. He could feel that this was his end. The administrative work gave him stress. He was isolated from his circle and did not want to interact with anybody. To avoid excess coughing, he talked less and communicated through orders in writing. He wrote a note on a piece of paper with a quill dipped in ink saying *Get me The Nine Unknown men.* His loyal minister read the note and left the King's royal residence. In an hour, nine men arrived in covered heads and were soon ushered towards the King's chambers. Once inside, they uncovered their heads and greeted the king by bowing heads.

Ashoka had not been to his chambers for a long time. He was living in an isolated bubble which was his royal residence. He refused to sit; he spoke long, stretched words with pauses. He spoke, "Gentlemen, or may I say—the Nine Unknown men, it has been decades, and this secret society has been doing well. I may die someday, this empire may die someday, but to ensure humanity does not die, this secret society must not die either. You and your successors in the near future will keep this secret society alive to keep humanity, your study, and your research alive. I give you my blessing to do well in keeping this society a secret and become a catalyst in making the world a better place. May God bless you!"

As The Nine Unknown men left his chambers, Ashoka lay on his bed and as he felt his time approaching, he chanted the mantra one final time and took his last few breaths,

"Buddham sharanam gacchami;

Sangam sharanam gacchami;

Dhamman sharanam gacchami."

Within a month, Ashoka died. His body was cremated, and fifty years after his reign, the Mauryan empire collapsed like a pack of cards. The last heir carrying the throne, Brihadhratha was assassinated by his military general Pushyamitra Shunga who later on established the Shunga dynasty and brought an end to the humongous and strong Mauryan empire. The great Mauryan empire faced its downfall, but the secret society of the Nine Unknown lives on to this very day.

# Part Two

# CHAPTER 5

**Modern-day India**
**More than two and a half millennia later**

Ananya Kulkarni is a student in her mid-twenties researching on her PhD subject—the "Connection of Secret Societies and Sociology". She is five-feet six inches tall, with light brown hair, a fair complexion, a button nose, and black eyes. Growing up, Ananya was quite fond of history and decided to actually pursue it unlike any of her friends or batchmates who took the conventional 9-5 corporate job. Ananya's grandmother would narrate to her stories of the Ramayana and the Mahabharata ever since she was twelve. In her teens, she developed her increasing love for history and with her skyrocketing perfect scores in social studies, and exclusively history, her grandmother gifted her a book every month or two. Her grandmother, who was a Doctorate, made her read books about the Ancient Indian history from the Mauryan dynasty in the North to the Chola dynasty in the South, then moving to the Ahom dynasty in the East, King Lalitaditya of Kashmir, and the Mahajanapadas of the West.

She was quite certain that her career must involve history. Her ambition was to become an archaeologist, but with the influence of Dan Brown's Dr. Robert Langdon series, she decided to row her boat towards a PhD on secret societies. Conspiracy theories always fascinated Ananya and research became her biggest skill alongside her deductive vision and razor-sharp memory which helped her remember dates easily. When she convinced her parents about pursuing the field of history, her parents supported her and her grandparents were more than delighted about her PhD research subject. Her parents were convinced about her strong language skills and her command over history. They assumed that she would make a great lawyer, but destiny had its own plans.

During her undergraduate days, her entire batch was filled with snobs and arrogant brats crowded around her. The people who were labelled nerds, geeks, or losers were drowned into their textbooks. Ananya did not belong to the faction of "My entire life revolves around studying" neither did she belong to the faction of "sex, drugs, and rock n' roll". After completing her BA in History, she went on to pursue her Masters in Ancient Indian History. Later on, she enrolled for a PhD programme where she met her mentor and guide Nivedita Kaur. Kaur and Ananya, in the beginning of the PhD programme would treat each other too formally and had a professional relationship. However, over due course of time, their relationship strengthened as the late night research work and the walks around the campus regarding various discussions came into the picture.

Kaur would give her week-long tasks to complete and Ananya would complete them over the course of a couple of days. One fine day, Ananya began her research about an ancient Indian secret society founded by King Ashoka the Great. She began her research with the Illuminati, then the Opus Dei, and after that, the Priory of Sion. She soon realised that she had researched on all the secret societies which were linked to Dan Brown's novels. She wanted to work on something unique till she came across India's very own secret society dating back to 250 BCE: The Nine Unknown founded by King Ashoka of the Mauryan dynasty. She asked her guide if she could conduct some research about Ashoka's Nine Unknown. Dr. Kaur was a little hesitant on approving something like that. She could not deny such a unique topic but did not approve of it either. She left a very moderate response of "We'll see," and proceeded to delegate her some more work to do. After two weeks of persistently failed persuasion, Ananya came up with an entire report that she had worked on over the weekend. Her room was filled with empty pizza boxes and coffee cups. On Monday, she reached a little late to the campus owing to some well-deserved sleep and handed over the report to Nivedita Kaur.

Ananya began her explanation, "This report includes everything that I should research on about the Nine Unknown.

I also researched on lesser-known links affiliated with The Nine Unknown. For example, I know that there is this one Buddhist library in Gaya which stores manuscripts written in the both old and advanced Prakrit and Pali languages about astrophysics and gravitational force. Or that there is another hidden library in a remote village on the outskirts of Dharamshala which has a door that has been locked for years and the board on it says that this library has been shifted to Kanakpura in Karnataka. But once you google this place, you see nothing but some cave. The Dharamshala library consist of all the scripts of Ashoka in the Pali and Prakrit languages."

Nivedita Kaur glanced at the report and saw each and every minute detail of the report that was created by her student. She was indeed very proud of her student and when Ananya saw the smile on her face, she was relieved thinking her project would finally be approved. Nivedita Kaur said, "I am really proud of you my child, believe me I really am. I don't say it to any of my students unless they reach a certain mark of excellence. When I see this report, I can say that this is a benchmark for the excellence one can achieve in the due course of forty-eight hours."

But, she paused for a moment wondering how Ananya could know about a hidden and locked library in Dharamshala that records Ashoka's manuscripts. Besides Kaur, there are only two other people who knew about this library and the cave in Kanakpura. There are very few people who have such rare information about Ashoka and the Nine Unknown, and

Ananya was one of them. She asked her Professor if The Nine Unknown really existed.

"This is good, but you didn't link the Nine Unknown with Sociology. You should join me over dinner at my house, so that we can peacefully discuss this. Take the day off. You deserve it kiddo!"

# CHAPTER-6

**8:30 p.m.**
**Nivedita Kaur's Residence**
**Sector 17, Gurgaon**
**Delhi**

Ananya travelled all the way from the DU campus to Sector 17 in Gurgaon to reach Nivedita Kaur's residence. She rang her bell, and there was Nivedita Kaur in a cooking apron greeting her with a smile and a warm, welcoming hug. It was a nice, small apartment filled with books, her research, her degree of bachelors in history, her PhD degree in Sociology, and some of her photos from college days where she had won multiple debate competitions. She lived alone inside her two-bedroom apartment. She was unmarried and had no child. She lived alone for a reason. Ananya wondered and asked, "Do you live alone, all by yourself?"

Kaur switched off the flame of her gas stove and started serving food on the table. As she served her a bowl of warm soup, she began, "I hope you enjoy it. Since you have been away from your family for quite a long time, I assumed you would love to have a good home-cooked meal."

"Certainly. The food is wonderful!" complimented Ananya.

"The reason why I called you here is because what I am about to tell you is extremely confidential. No one should *ever* know about this information. It is a *secret*!" said Kaur.

Ananya nodded. Kaur paused for a few seconds and said,

"I am a part of the ancient secret society founded by King Ashoka called The Nine Unknown."

"Are you serious? You're joking right?" chuckled Ananya.

"Why would I invite you over my place then?" asked Kaur in a rhetorical manner as she laid back on to her wooden chair.

"Most certainly not to tell me you are a part of the Nine Unknown!" said Ananya sarcastically.

"This is a serious matter Ananya. So to answer your question from the morning, yes—the Nine Unknown exists on to this day," Kaur revealed.

"Well, I knew that the Nine Unknown existed because of that one online article by the Newsbird. I didn't expect you to be a part of it!" Ananya exclaimed.

"You must have done a lot of digging into this matter then. I must give you better marks for good research in that case," Kaur smiled.

"So let's talk about this then, after all now we both know that this kind of a cult or a club, or some gang does exists."

"Not a cult. It is a secret society!" Kaur corrected her fellow student.

"Sorry, a *secret society*. I did a bit of a research on The Nine Unknown; however, I did not understand was that there have been multiple wars, economic crisis, and outbreaks. So, why has the Nine Unknown not offerred its help when they had infinite knowledge and ancient wisdom for help?" Ananya asked.

"You have a valid point right there. The thing is that whenever we feel the time is right to reveal these studies, we do it, but secretly. You see it in the news about a new study being published by scientists or a cure for some possible outbreak or anything similar. We are the ones who reveal this information to the right people secretly. If we hand it to the wrong hands then that would be worse for humanity," Kaur explained about the secret society she was a part of.

Nivedita went back to her small kitchen making two cups of warm, frothy coffee. Both of them sat on a blue comfortable couch with coffee mugs in their hands. Ananya sipped her coffee, the smell was sweet and the taste of the coffee topped up with heavy and creamy milk gave pure joy to her taste buds. She smiled and complimented, "The coffee is wonderful. I love it. Thank you ma'am!"

The two resumed back to their conversation. Ananya asked, "What were the subjects the Nine Unknown were supposed to study?"

"Each of the nine were given a subject to research, revise, and update their work. The subjects were: Propaganda,

Physiology, Microbiology, Alchemy, Communication, Gravity, Cosmology, Light, and Sociology," Kaur continued.

"What is your subject of research in that case?" asked Ananya curiously.

"Sociology. Considering the fact that I do have a PhD in that," Kaur answered.

"The real question is why are you telling me all of this and is there anyone else who knows apart from me?" Ananya asked.

"You were the one student in my entire teaching career, spanning more than forty years, who could understand and conduct research extraordinarily. What you have uncovered in doing so—about the library in Dharamshala—is something no one else apart from the Nine Unknown is aware of. Moreover, you are passionate and curious. You have become my favourite student over the years. So Ananya, you must know the weight of my trust on you—you are now a part of something really big."

Ananya claimed, "I do love history. I have been wanting to learn about Indian history ever since the tales told by my grandmother and the books she made me read."

"In that case, your grandmother did a great job."

Ananya said, "Not to brag, but ever since my school days, I have aced history and I was always top of the class. My friends from school kept asking me about how I got good grades all the time. It was just my love for history. They also asked me about the whole point of learning history, that's a question I never got an answer to."

Ananya's professor answered, "History should be studied as real stories from the past that help us understand what kind of a person we should be and what we should not be for the present and the near future."

Ananya used this opportunity to genuinely praise her professor, "Thank you so much for answering that question ma'am. I really look up to you as a mentor to me and you have taught me a lot of things."

"I have to give you three things that you must keep with yourself."

Professor Kaur walked inside her study and removed three things from her wardrobe. First was a briefcase with a digitally-crypted lock, second was a golden key, and third was a book carved with the Ashokan lion and SOCIOLOGY written under the lion seal on a brown-leathered cover. She gave a different key to Ananya. "You will like this once you become a part of a game of mystery...of history. The Nine Unknown may have been compromised. So never give this key to anyone. I mean NO ONE," warned the professor as her light-green eyes were about to pop out.

Professor Kaur smiled and showered kind words of wisdom on her student, "Take refuge in the path of knowledge, spread the knowledge you have, and make knowledge your duty. May God bless you my child."

Ananya finished her cup of coffee and decided to leave. As she walked towards the door of the apartment, Kaur warned her, "Never tell anyone about what I told you. Act as if we never had this conversation."

Ananya replied smartly in agreeing to Kaur's concerned warning, "What conversation? I was never here in the first place."

She walked outside her building; it was completely dark. A rustle of a few leaves made her turn back as if she heard the footsteps of someone. She saw nothing and assumed it to be the wind. She walked to her two wheeler, wore her helmet, and started her vehicle at lightning speed to avoid any trouble at night in Delhi. As she reached her hostel building, the main gate was locked from the inside. She had no other option but to climb through one of the walls or else she would have to spend the night outside in the cold month of November.

She put her phone in her tight jeans. She firmly tied the laces of her sneakers and took a heighted jump on the wall. She jumped over the wall and landed with her elbow on one big and pointy rock that hurt her ribs. She was grunting in pain. She had succeeded in getting inside but still had to sneak into her room slowly. The guard was still snoring despite a big thud approximately 10 yards in front of him. Ananya saw a padlock on the door of the hostel. She had to steal the keys from the snoring guard's cabin. She slowly removed the key from the key holder without making any noise and took silent and slow footsteps to not wake the guard up. She unlocked the padlock and went back to the cabin to return the key back in the key holder. Then she swiftly and stealthily went towards her room where her roommate was still awake, scrolling through Instagram reels. Ananya was long bored of reels and felt that it is a complete waste of time that reduces attention span. She walked inside the room swiftly acting like she was never out of it.

Her roommate asked, "Where were you at this time? Isn't the gate closed?"

"I was taking a stroll outside," answered Ananya with a much calm and composed manner.

"But shouldn't the gate be closed? We are supposed to be inside our dorms at nine, asleep, and it is 10:30 already," her roommate enquired as she looked at her phone to check the time.

"But are we sleeping?" argued Ananya.

Her roommate pulled her blanket, switched off the lights, and closed her eyes after the endless reels-scrolling on Instagram. Ananya was still awake in her sleep reflecting back on the long conversation over dinner at her history professor's place. Her professor was a part of an ancient secret society of King Ashoka the Great. A part of a secret society with information so potent that could change the world to either a utopia or a horrible dystopia. Was Ananya supposed to feel excited or worried? Good or bad? She had no clue. She closed her eyes and retired the day to her sleep. But the coffee made by her favourite professor did not let her sleep and kept her awake as she questioned what all had happened in the past hour.

# CHAPTER 7

**The Next Morning**
**Dean's Office**
**The College Campus**
**Delhi**

Morning, 8:30 a.m. Ananya woke up from her sleep. Her roommate wasn't there and neither was her bag. In a matter of minutes, she got ready for college and stepped down to the ground floor—the lobby of the girl's hostel. She noticed the padlock still sitting on the ground, covered in dust, even though the guard was awake. Ananya walked faster, heading towards her department's building carrying the name board of "Department of Social Studies". She walked inside the building, towards her classroom. An hour went by, but her professor did not arrive. She checked her calendar to see if Ancient Indian History with Nivedita Kaur was in her today's timetable or not. Turns out she was right, but her professor was not present. Just then, the college dean walked into the classroom and ordered, "Ananya Kulkarni, come to my office right away!"

Ananya could sense something troublesome. Either she caused it or something was about to happen to her or maybe both of them. She slowly walked behind the dean who seemed to be very worried and angry. As she walked from the department building to the administrative office where the dean's office or what the students called "the dean's den" is located. Walking on the concrete road of the campus, they noticed an ambulance passing by them with the sirens on. She wondered what must have happened.

After some walking, the dean who was an economics professor, and Ananya were seated in her office. The Dean's arthritis made it challenging for her to walk properly, hence she was limping. Ananya sat down and could feel butterflies in her stomach for two reasons: a.) The anxiety of punishment coming her way, b.) she was also hungry as she had skipped breakfast today. She usually loved breakfast but had it while skipping her second lecture on Industrial Revolution in European History paper which was also her minor subject in her undergraduate course, a topic in history she found boring.

Which brought her to this time at 9:47 a.m. The college dean growled, "Do you know what has happened here?"

"No," said Ananya.

"Where were you last night?" the Dean asked another question as she opened her iPad.

"In my room inside the hostel," Ananya replied hesitantly.

"Are you sure?" asked the principal, giving a death stare and tapping a few times on her iPad.

"Yeah. I was there in my room at 9 p.m.," Ananya spoke with more confidence the second time.

"Then how do you explain me this," the Dean, placed her iPad in front of Ananya, playing the CCTV footage of Ananya sneaking inside the girl's hostel. "You lied to me. And now you have to explain to me what have you done to Nivedita Kaur."

"I didn't do anything to her. Yes, I was there at her house, and we were just having a normal conversation. Nothing else."

"Don't fool me. Do you know what happened to Professor Kaur?" asked the shouting Dean. "She has died and there were traces of blood in her apartment. She has been murdered and the police has taken her body for autopsy."

Ananya was shocked, completely taken aback. She felt as if she were punched in the stomach with that bad news. It was last night, hardly twelve hours ago or so that they had been discussing about The Nine Unknown, a secret that she felt she must not reveal to anyone ever. She spoke slowly but firmly, with confidence, "Ma'am. I did go to Professor Kaur's house but it was only to discuss about my history assignment and nothing else. She invited me to dinner, and all we chatted about was the current topic we were working on. I needed some of her guidance. I did not kill her, and it is a very shocking news for me to go through, considering that my favourite professor has been murdered."

The Dean nodded her head. Ananya started shedding a few tears from her eyes. The Dean offered Ananya a box of tissues and she wiped her tears. She could feel that Ananya was telling the truth, but not the entire truth. She let her leave and take the day off.

As she walked towards the main area where most students hang out, a stranger approached her and gave her a small bag. He moved so swiftly, before she could see his face, he had disappeared. She checked the bag, and it contained a small phone and only one contact number to dial in. She dialled the number and a robotic voice spoke to her, "Ananya, if you want to know who killed Nivedita Kaur, then meet me at that café near your campus at 11:30 a.m." Ananya checked her smartwatch which was showing 10:39 a.m. already. She is less than an hour away from meeting these anonymous people. At this moment she was freaked out yet curious to know what was about to happen. It was only a matter of time.

# CHAPTER-8

**11:30 a.m.**
**A nearby Cafe**
**Moti Baug**
**Delhi**

Ananya walked inside the said café near the campus. Suddenly, a man with his face covered in a pair of light brown shades and a mask appeared, and gave her a paper bag. Surprised, she examined the bag and looked back to see where the guy was, but he vanished into thin air. There was a page with a long note. Ananya donned her Sherlockian hat and felt the texture of handmade paper along with the smell of a fountain ink pen. She read the note written in an immaculate handwriting:

*To avoid any digital footprints traceability, I had to send this letter. Come to the Aristocrat's Hotel near Patel Nagar tomorrow in the evening at 7:30 p.m.; meet me at the Café in the lobby. Do not tell anyone about this as this is supposed to be strictly confidential. Your life is in danger and we are here to help you, provided that you also help us. Until then, see you tomorrow.*

She read the letter and did not know what to do and where to go. Should she go back to college? What if someone was going to harm her there? Should she go back home? What if someone was already putting a watch on her? Should she go to the hotel? What if they were ready to kill her once she reached. But the real question she forgot to answer in a quick flash of multiples was: who were these people who called her and sent her a handwritten note too? Could it be the murderer of Nivedita Kaur? Could it be The Nine Unknown? She was so worried and tensed about it, that she could not wait anymore to find out.

She was just a day away to find out why her life was in danger, and who was this person that sent this letter to her. Who was trying to kill her, and was it the same person who killed Nivedita Kaur? She had multiple questions in her head and wanted to control them. She was desperately searching for a meaning, for answers. Ananya tried to calm herself, and suppress her anxiety. All she had to do was wait for a day to find out what was to happen, and till then, she was supposed to not say a word to anyone about the Nine Unknown, Nivedita Kaur, or the note she received from an anonymous person. She headed back to her hostel dorm room. She was still chanting the mantra at the back of her mind to calm herself and thought of distracting herself with something till tomorrow evening.

# CHAPTER 9

**2:00 a.m.**
**Aristocrat's Hotel**
**Patel Nagar**
**Delhi**

There were nine people. Some old, some young but all of them belonged to the same organisation. One of them was a fairly young gentleman named Mark Tanner. A young Brit, graduate in Economics and History from Eton University, who later on pursued his dream of working for the MI6. After fifteen years of working for Her Majesty's Secret Service, he got the opportunity to look over the security and the information of the Nine Unknown. He had a strong security network everywhere he went.

And then, for the finances—the members chip in 40% of the money they earn, which was sufficient enough for the staff. The Nine Unknown, as an organisation did have someone they consider as an associate—who does not participate in their work per se, but is always be on the lookout for them or any other person who could join the Nine Unknown. So people like Mark Tanner were not a part of the Nine Unknown directly but were associated with it indirectly for the sake of logistics and security.

The entire suite was filled with the Nine Unknown and three other men who were with Tanner. Mark began, "It is quite late, now that we have all arrived through our last minute flights to India, to Delhi, at this hour. But we did it for a loss. A massive loss for all of us. I had a man on the inside who told me that the autopsy reports claim that she was killed and so do the evidences. Yes, my sources also sneaked inside her apartment and it is certain that there was a murder weapon and also a lot of blood. Who killed her? And why? These are questions we are too late to answer. It is today that we mourn an important member of the Nine, and we will never stop grieving but we have to move on. Tomorrow, we are going to be at the funeral. She hasn't been cremated yet because there are some formalities to be done like contact her family and all of that."

An old lady who was a part of the Nine asked, "Do we know who is going to replace her?"

"No, not yet. However, we have started our research and are on the lookout," said Mark.

The suite was taken over by shadow of silence, grief, and shock. Mark continued, "After the funeral, we will also have a new person coming at this hotel. We have been keeping a watch on her for a while since we have also been keeping an eye on Kaur." Mark took a pause to realise that the present tense should be changed to the past tense. "*Had*, kept a watch on Kaur. This person has also been accused as a suspect, and we believe that we could get something out of her."

An eighty-year old man growled, blowing his moustache and rough beard, "On what grounds do you allow this person to come here?"

"Nivedita Kaur had mentioned her once in our quarterly meetings, saying she had this one student who does most of the research for her. Kaur said she can trust her, and as I mentioned, since we have been keeping a watch on her, she mentioned about the Nine Unknown, about us, the day before yesterday's lecture with Kaur. Since my people keep a watch on Kaur and all of you here, you all know that I get the usual reports every week. She mentioned yesterday that we had been mentioned in the class and assured us with full confidence that this student is very trustable. She has excellent research skills has been a loyal student. And you guys know for a fact that Nivedita is very hard to please, and to earn her trust is like climbing Everest. So if she says so, then it has to be true."

Another woman from the Nine Unknown asked, "You said someone killed her. Does that mean we could become the potential next targets too?"

"Yes. There is a risk of one of us being dead next. But do not worry, I am here, and there is nothing to worry about at all. We believe that this student of hers can be of use to us."

The Nine Unknown all retired to their allotted rooms, arranged for them by Mark—including the flight tickets and other transportation. There was grief and worry. Grief for their lost colleague, and worry for the danger coming at them.

# CHAPTER 10

**The Library**
**University Campus**

Ananya walked inside the library with her bag. She paced towards the corner of the library and quietly opened her bag. She stared at small black box containing the golden key. Closing the box sitting on the bag, she kept it inside the bag. The library was quiet and it had only a few professors/ students sitting in different corners of the library. While some students were browsing through different shelves scouting for some books, there were some diligent, overtly studious students too, sitting with their stationery and a huge pile of books. Professors worked quietly in the library as it was quite peaceful and silent. They could also refer to the books in the library, if needed. The entire environment of the library was so quiet that professors preferred working in the middle of this sea of bookshelves rather than sitting in the staffroom filled with gossip about almost every other student, professor, celebrity, and whatnot.

Ananya unzipped her bag and opened a file with a brown leather cover. The label of the file on brown cardboard paper was stamped—CONFIDENTIAL in capital red letters. The last time she met her mentor Nivedita Kaur, she was handed a few things to keep safe with her. Among other things, there was also a file that had all the information about the Nine Unknown. Ananya opened the file which contained all the profiles and the background information of each member of the Nine Unknown and began reading it.

Starting with Dr. Leena Gokhale, a Doctorate in Chemistry from Bombay University, now called Mumbai University. She had received multiple awards for her research and has been cited in multiple books, research journals, and research papers for her work in chemistry. She lived in Delhi with her daughter, grandchildren, and her husband, who has retired from his college professorship. He too worked in the same academic field. In the daytime, she is this wonderful and loving grandmother, but when the sun sets, she stayed up till 2:00 a.m. to work on her research for the Nine. Her field in the secret society: Alchemy.

Then there is Rupert Roy, he was working in the field of journalism since the age of 15, when the second world war was happening. He joined the frontline with his gun, an old camera, a notebook, and a pen. That is how his journalism career had started. Later on, he made cartoons and created propaganda in multiple countries—leading to controversies, assassinations, civil wars, conventional wars, and whatnot. This is because Rupert Roy had been doing his work under the pen-name: Purret, which is just Rupert jumbled-up. Roy had been a senior and celebrated journalist. Whenever he was brought to the spotlight and asked controversial questions, he always replied in a polite and diplomatic tone. However, he has been studying Propaganda for years now, and has reached some solutions to prevent or tackle propaganda. Why is it caused and in what way can propaganda be used for the right reasons? And how would the evil minds use propaganda in their favour which could lead to the unimaginable? All this was his subject of study: Propaganda.

After that, Ananya turned the page to see the next profile of Dr. Ashwin Tripathi who hailed from Lucknow. He completed his MBBS post-graduation in Physiology from the Columbia Medical School. Ashwin became a physician and a surgeon who had an expertise in surgery of the human anatomy. After spending about two decades as a surgeon, Ashwin Tripathi pursued a PhD in Physiology and the human anatomy from the University of Edinburgh. Considering his expertise, his subject of study was: Physiology.

Then was Paula Maxwell; she used to be a part of the American Society of Microbiology for more than twenty years. A Harvard graduate, her work in Microbiology gave her recognition as a famous microbiology researcher, and also the opportunity to use her study for a good cause by being a part of the Nine Unknown. To mention some things about her personal life: She lived in Seattle, Washington in the United States, in her penthouse apartment. She worked in her private laboratory. She had a daughter living in New York pursuing law as a part of her post-graduation course from the University of Columbia. She divorced her husband a decade ago as he assaulted and abused her. Paula's various research works gives her a seat in the secret society in the field: Microbiology.

Next, Ananya saw the profile of Tobey Fox, he came from a small town in Philadelphia. He had majored in Communications from the UCLA Berkeley for his masters and did Astrophysics for his undergrad. He later pursued his career in mass media and appeared in a few news networks as a well-known news anchor and journalist. He was a bachelor in his mid-30s, and after working in media for a decade, he recieved an offer from the Nine Unknown to do his research on communication. He does not have much to share in fact. He has this introverted and reserved personality, and focused on his research by not speaking much. His subject of study: Communications.

Ananya turned another page to see Shilpa Dixit, hailing from Delhi as an army kid. She was interested in joining the Armed Forces, but her family refrained her. Yet, because of her good grades in sciences, she chose to study about astrophysics, astronomy, the cosmos—the space. She had done multiple important projects in organisations like the European Space Agency, ISRO, and NASA. Wherever there was some research, discovery or something or the other related to the cosmos, her name would instantly pop-up which gave her recognition to The Nine Unknown who were on the hunt for an astrophysics or space scientist. Nivedita Kaur, Leena Gokhale, and Shilpa Dixit have been great friends over the time, starting as colleagues. Each of their circles was aware of their friendship but little did they know that they are colleagues and members of an ancient secret society. She has a husband who is a retired government official and a son who is studying in IIT Mumbai. Her subject of study: Cosmology.

Next to Dixit's profile was a German name—Stefan Schmidt. Hailing from the town of Frankfurt, Schmidt was interested and fascinated about light. Like Albert Einstein, he too wondered—what is light? He was on the quest of knowing more about light and got into an electrical engineering course in Munich. Whenever he looked at light, he wondered what it must be made of? He believed and wondered that light could be more than just electromagnetic radiation visible to the human eye. He always looked at the rays of the sunlight, the man-made tube light, and wondered if it is something more than what meets the eye. He had done such deep research over the last five years about light, even quitting his job as an electrical engineer; he decided to follow his childhood curiosity. This news was brought to The Nine Unknown and Schmidt, a man in his forties who studied for his innate human curiosity now decided to research for the benefit of humanity. His childhood curiosity became his subject of study in the secret society: Light.

And finally, Ananya glanced through the profile of Isaac Joseph: born in the Caribbean, he was really interested in physics. He was a shy and silent person who was not much of a talker. He simply read books about physics. Coincidentally, he shared the name with the father of physics: Isaac Newton. He got a scholarship in UCLA where he remained a good student and simply studied physics and got even more fascinated by it. He had a home in Santa Clara, lived with a wife and two sons in middle school. His research papers, books, and articles on physics lead him to his subject of study in the secret society: Gravity.

All of the Nine Unknown were appointed with an intense and deep background check done by Tanner and his people. Based on that, the offer of joining The Nine Unknown was given to a certain someone who had qualified credentials to study and research on their subject of expertise and were able to keep it a secret. Then, the job was given to the best fit who was perfect and most trustworthy candidate to join the secret society. Working for the Nine Unknown did not give you much money. In fact, most of them were college professors, PhD guides, consultants, or journalists. The members of the Nine Unknown regularly chipped in certain amount of money to gather funds for themselves and for their work.

# CHAPTER 11

**An Unknown Mansion**
**Hampshire**
**London**

"The head of the Nine has been killed, the Remaining Eight of us are here in Delhi for her funeral. The funeral is tomorrow in the afternoon around 2 p.m. and we are leaving at night for the Delhi Airport. We'll take our flight and then head to our respective homes."

"Sounds like a plan," said a deep voice. "But there is going to be a change of plans. Before any of them even makes it to the airport tomorrow, all of you will die the night of the funeral."

"Nothing should happen to me. I have received my money at the cost of the information I provided, which is why I should not be killed," said an old voice on the phone adding more force to the statement.

"Sure. I will send my man to your hotel rooms. You will be escorted by my man after the Remaining Seven are killed."

"Also, there is this one girl who is a student of that oldie Nivedita. She is coming in here tomorrow."

"What for?" said the deep voice with a tone of concern.

"Mark says she is a favourite student of Nivedita, and that is why she is here. She did the research for Nivedita's study."

"We will kill her too...or...we could use her..."

The deep voice disconnects the call.

The mansion was made in an old-fashioned brickwork in an English countryside with a typical British–European form of architecture in the Hampshire county. Inside the mansion was a long room seating five people. The deep voice was none other than the British billionaire and business mogul, Richard Burton. Along with him, there was the American media entrepreneur, Kenny Roman. Resting comfortably on a chair was the Indian scientist, Lalit Bakshi; along with him was another Russian space scientist, Dmitri Baladin. A German physicist named Tobias Schneider enjoying his cup of tea and a Chinese light engineer named Yao Zhi brewing his cup of tea. All of them were sitting in one room. Richard Burton begun, "We have one dead in our hand, and her books have been stolen. Now we will kill them all and then snatch their research."

The ones sitting inside the mansion room were all called the Sword of Power. Each and every one of them came together for one reason: power, already reflecting in the name. Richard Burton, Kenny Roman, Lalit Bakshi, Dmitri Baladin, Tobias Schneider, and Yao Zhi joined hands to gain the highest level of knowledge, to be used for gaining more power. The power which in the wrong hands, can cause destruction. But there was the fear of The Nine Unknown. The Sword of Power's purpose was to hunt down and kill each and every member of King Ashoka's ancient secret society. Then, steal all of their research only to use the pious study for their selfish intentions. The motive of Sword of Power is to get their hands on the valuable knowledge of their respective favourite fields, and then manipulate and exploit the research. Their power-lust goes to the extent of controlling the entire world on their fingertips. The Sword of Power is a dangerous organisation with possibly twice the funding than The Nine Unknown.

The Sword of Power sent one of their own contract killer, his codename: Orion, who is also the strongest of the mercenaries funded by the Sword of Power. He was the one who killed Nivedita Kaur. Burton rang Orion on his phone using a scrambler which would prevent location tracking.

"Orion, I just spoke with Purret, you know what is to be done."

"Yes, I will. I just need my money and I will do the damn job well."

"You will. I am sending a six-figure amount as an untraceable transaction to your bank account. I just need them dead."

"Also Hercules," Orion referred to Burton's codename. "There this one girl who is a student of Nivedita Kaur. I am going to convince her into working for us, I will tell her that the SOP is the new Nine Unknown. She will work for us, and once the job is done we will kill her."

"Great plan, just don't make a mess or else one mistake can completely fry us."

Burton had always been curious about The Nine Unknown. His famous agency, the News Bird once ran a story on Ashoka and decided to make a documentary on him where Burton himself was the anchor. However, during the process of research, he found an online news article about The Nine Unknown. He got into deep research about this secret society and ended up planning out a way to steal all their research and destroy it. He decided to team up with those who could study the subjects of The Nine Unknown, and Burton paid them a heavy amount to board them on this plan. Burton coaxed them into believing that this was a good cause, beneficial to all of them. But, he planned to use all others as pawns, so that he could grow on to hold the entire world's power in his rich, powerful, selfish, and evil hands.

# CHAPTER 12

**4:00 a.m.**
**An Old-fashioned Apartment**
**Old Delhi**

Ishir, a tall, bulky, muscular man with a sharp beard. His name suited him perfectly; Ishir—as powerful and strong as fire. He had served in the Indian army as a captain. He was married and gifted with a kid, his life was perfect for him until one day, he got heavily injured in a paramilitary operation due to a malfunction with his parachute. He broke his left leg with a broken heel near the tibia bone and had to get screws attached to fix his heavily injured shoulder. He had to leave the army for a year after facing multiple injuries. When he returned, the first operation in the paramilitary was one where he was close to reaching the Major rank. He was shot with three bullets on his back. He survived but was forced to retire from the army. His lifelong dream came to a sudden end because of the injuries he faced.

After being forced to retire from the Indian military, he faced multiple financial issues piercing his heart like bullets when enough bullets had caused him emotional and psychological damages. With all the chaos happening, his wife divorced him for not being present for them and also the lack of providing for the family. She got the custody of her son: Ishaan. The sad man turned angry, and to make some good money and vent out all the anger, he soon joined a group called the Wolf's Claw where he became the commander and led the group. The Wolf's Claw was supposed to hunt down, kidnap, or even liquidate mafias, dirty politicians, government officers, intelligence agents, terrorists, and all the evil people who misused their power to harm innocent beings. The government of multiple countries would hire the Wolf's Claw for their service, and they would get six-figure payments for it. The military of the countries they were on an assignment for, could easily be noticed but the Wolf's Claw was a private organisation which was not even official. From murdering mafias in Cuba to assassinating Army officials in Pakistan to bombing terrorist camps in Afghanistan and Syria. Ishir brought back his life from a harmful injury and a heartbreaking divorce to an adventure of the Robin Hood in a dark, violent environment, raining bullets and blood. As of now, he plans to chase the Nine Unknown for preserving an ancient secret. However, he is not after the Nine Unknown, he is looking for a person named Orion, and the organisation paying him for this assignment is Her Majesty's Secret Service: the MI6.

Ishir played a call recording between Orion and the Sword of Power. He traced the location of the call, which turned out to be the Aristocrat's Hotel. He heard the mention of Kaur's student reaching the hotel at 7:30 p.m. Ishir planned a way to get inside the Aristocrat's and kill Orion. He could not even rest his eyes for a minute as the adrenaline did not let him sleep.

# CHAPTER 13

**The Next Morning**
**A Nearby Crematorium**

The priest was chanting a few mantras. Nivedita Kaur's body had been drenched in oil and her nephew lit the pyre which started burning. Ananya was sad, she could not hold back her tears. Suddenly, Mark Tanner appeared putting his hand on her shoulder to console her saying, "Everything will be alright." Ananya wondered who this man was. His blue eyes were covered with his dark shades, and she could smell the fragrance of an expensive perfume he was wearing. She asked, "Who are you? Do you know Professor Nivedita?"

Mark whispered, "Yes, I work with her. You are meeting me at 7:30 in the evening today. See you there." Ananya wondered what he was talking about. She pondered if this man was a part of the Nine Unknown. She turned back to glance but the man had disappeared. He was nowhere to be seen. However, the remaining people of the secret society were present, grieving for their colleague. For Dr. Leena Gokhale and Shilpa Dikshit, Nivedita Kaur was more than just a colleague. She was a great friend of theirs.

She decided to face whatever is going to happen once she meets this person at 7:30 p.m. at the Aristocrat's Hotel. She was getting anxious and worried about the risk that she could face. A risk to her life and possibly a risk to her family. Ananya was worried and wanted a distraction to get away from a depressing funeral and an overthinking mind. She ran away from the crematorium and walked. She kept walking till she saw a park where she sat on a bench. She took out her earphones and started listening to music on her phone. Some calming music really stopped her from overthinking. She was all set to head to the hotel in the evening.

# CHAPTER 14

**The same evening**
**7:30 p.m.**
**Aristocrat's Hotel**
**Patel Nagar**
**Delhi**

Ananya walked inside the hotel where she was greeted by a tall gentleman wearing a suit with well-groomed hair who was sitting at the café on the ground floor, which was right next to the hotel lobby. This gentleman asked in his deep voice, "Hi Ananya, do you remember we met this morning?"

"Yes, I remember."

"Come along with me. We are going upstairs."

The man escorted her to the elevator and pressed the button which led them to the floor where the Remaining Eight were seated in their suite. Tanner knocked on the door of one of the suites and reminded one of the members to head to his suite, where he was staying. Ananya wondered who were these people, Tanner was knocking the room doors of? She strongly believed that they were none other than the Nine Unknown.

Tanner walked from the rooms towards his suite. Noticing this, Ananya followed him. Tanner removed the key card from the breast pocket of his formal jacket and swiped through the suite door censor. Tanner opened the door for Ananya to walk inside. He noticed the members of the nine walking towards his suite. He held the door till all of them were inside. The only one remaining was Tobey Fox. A few minutes after everyone had settled, Tobey barged in smelling of alcohol, he was drunk about an hour ago which is why he is holding a hot cup of coffee to possibly try adding some energy to his brain.

Everyone stared at Tobey. Tanner began, "Alright everyone, the reason I called everyone to this room was because I have to introduce you all to someone. Her name is Ananya Kulkarni, Nivedita Kaur's student. She is the one who is going to help us."

Ananya stared at him for a moment, wondering what on Earth is wrong with Tanner. How can she be of any help to Tanner? "Excuse me mister. Why on Earth do you require my help? I'm sorry but I can't be a part of your secret society. I am a PhD student, and I have absolutely no interest in being a part of this just because my professor was in it and I was her favourite student."

Tanner proposed a point, "Your favourite professor recommended you. She trusted you. You can keep up to that promise, can you?"

Ananya closed her eyes, took a deep breath. She remembered the dinner with her professor, and wiped a tear running from her eye. Leena Gokhale, who was sitting next to the standing Ananya, patted her back for her to calm down. She could understand her feelings as Ananya's history professor was her colleague and best friend. She whispered, "It is okay to feel like this. We all know this feeling." Tanner opened a bottle of water on the dining table, he poured the water in a glass and offered it to her. As she gulped down the water, she felt a little lighter and calmer. She wiped her tears and her upper lip. She said, "I will do it. But do we know who killed her?"'

Tanner briefly stated, "We don't know but we are investigating. Right now, I would suggest that all of you head someplace safe because if one of us is dead, then chances are that all of us will be targeted. We all are going to the Mehrauli house in Delhi, where you guys are going to live for the time being. Pack your bags now, we will be heading out tomorrow morning after breakfast."

The drunk Tobey was taking some time after finishing his coffee to actually register what was going on in this suite and what was everyone talking about.

"Do I need to pack my bag?"

"No, just grab your laptop, your books, your notes. Basically whatever is required for your research. Your clothes and essentials will be taken care of."

Ananya walked towards the door. Tanner ordered the Remaining Eight members to start packing their bags right away. Ananya and Tanner took the elevator to the lobby, from there the both of them walked towards the parking lot of the hotel. Tanner opened the door for Ananya as she sat in and then sat on the driver's seat to start the car to visit her college. There was still some time for the curfew to end. It was not supposed to be the usual traffic. It was a bit more quieter which is why Tanner drove the car at an increased speed. Within 15 minutes they reached the college gate. Ananya sprinted towards the hostel gate as fast as she could.

After reaching, she took a few deep breaths to calm down. She rushed towards her room. Her roommate was not inside. She grabbed her laptop bag and put in her laptop, chargers, Air Pods. She grabbed her textbooks and opened this massive box filled with files that were packed with all her notes and research work based on the assignments given by her professor. She stuffed all of those things inside. She donned a purple-coloured hoodie and wore white-coloured sneakers. After throwing in some sanitary pads in case of emergency, she finally donned the straps of her laptop backpack and plonked from the staircase again rushing towards Tanner's vehicle—a giant minivan.

As Ananya sat in, she said, "I have packed absolutely everything that is needed." Tanner nodded, "Great. We start work from now on." He told, "Delete all your social media platforms. Who knows who must be tracking you." She replied, "I don't have any social media." Tanner stared at her for a second, then drove off the car to head back to the hotel.

* * *

Ishir walked inside the hotel main gate. He casually walked past the security check and even through the lobby gate. A security guard reminded him to stand near the security scanner. He defended himself by lying, "I live here. I got myself checked in about a few days ago." The security let him go which made him walk through the lobby door. He walked towards the receptionist and asked her, "May I know if there has been an Englishman who checked in at this hotel, let's say approximately 48 hours ago?"

The receptionist checked her screen and said, "Yes sir, there are two."

"What are the names if I may know? There's this friend of mine who I know is staying here, and I want to surprise him," asked Ishir leaving a cheeky smile.

"There is a Mr. Mark Tanner living in room 1086."

"Thank you. Don't call Mr. Tanner's room, I want to surprise him," Ishir said a believable lie to the receptionist. He took out his phone and messaged someone on his phone. He texted "Orion on Site". Following up with another message, "I will keep you posted."

Ishir walked inside the elevator and presses the floor on which room 1086 was situated. After a few seconds, the elevator doors slid out through which Ishir walked out. Ishir pulled out a small pistol and removed a cylindrical tube known as a silencer to suppress the noise of the gun. He attached the silencer to the muzzle (the barrel or the mouth of the pistol from which bullets release) of the gun whipped out from his leather jacket's zipped front pocket. He moved ahead and looked for Room 1086. After some looking around and stealthily walking. He finally saw the sign of Room 1086.

Ishir pulled out his small pistol. He could hear murmurs. Ishir had not seen Orion before. He knew his name, his details, and his codename. Ishir stuck his ear to the door to overhear, he heard a British accent murmuring, "The Preserver of the Nine Unknown's secrets and research could be in possible danger. We must save him after we have grabbed our current works. You have your files with you right now and the ones sent to me a month ago are at the safehouse." Ishir identified the British accent and hid his gun under his t-shirt. He knocked on the door of the room. Tanner immediately turned towards the door. Tanner grabbed his gun from the drawer near his bed and tucked it on the back of his shirt. He opened the door and looked at Ishir wearing bulky shoes and a leather jacket. Ishir said, "Seems like I walked into the wrong room," Tanner smiled in slight relief and replied, "Yeah seems like it mate." He noticed the British accent and walked a step closer. Ishir swiftly pushed his hand on Tanner's chest till Tanner's back hit the door. Tanner pushed Ishir with all his might towards the wall of the floor's corridor. Ishir's head hit the wall and he fell. Tanner removed his gun and smacked the back of his head using the bottom of his gun which made Ishir unconscious. Tanner rushed inside his room and ordered the members of the secret society, "Grab the bags that contain your work and let's get the hell out of here before this man does anything to us. Meet me in the lobby. Hurry up now!"

The eight members of the secret society rushed out of Tanner's suite towards their own hotel rooms in a hurry to grab all of their work. They did not bother carrying much of their clothes and other essentials as that was not their top priority. Tanner grabbed a suitcase and a briefcase. He told Ananya to grab her bag and run away from his room towards the lobby. Ananya set her foot outside the room door and ran swiftly towards the elevator where the other members were present. She hopped inside the elevator along with the members of The Nine. The elevator's capacity was seven people so she had to step away till Tanner came.

Meanwhile, Tanner was packing his stuff together. He glanced at Ishir who had slightly opened his eyes facing the open hotel room door. Ishir noticed Tanner putting a silencer to the pistol that he tucked to his back. While Tanner was rolling the silencer to his pistol's muzzle. Ishir, without making any noise, stealthily scurried away to the emergency exit. Tanner added a white cubic solid which happened to look like sugar inside that cup of coffee that Tobey was sipping on.

Mark Tanner walked out of his room after getting his things, with his pistol in his left hand. He looked around for that man who came here to assault them. He holstered the gun inside his formal jacket and walked towards the elevator where he joined Ananya inside it to reach the ground floor. Tanner placed his suitcase around the lounge area of the hotel lobby and ran towards the parking space to get his car. He asked each and every one of the Nine to give him their research work which are all in briefcases. Dr. Gokhale sensed something odd with Tanner. She decided to remove a box from her briefcase and hid it with herself before handing over the briefcase to Mark. Tanner carefully placed each briefcase inside the trunk of his SUV. Rupert and Dr. Leena Gokhale who were standing near the car asked him why was he keeping these briefcases with him inside the car.

Tanner said, "I will take these briefcases with me to a secure location. Then I will go to his holiness and take the manuscripts from him." Leena sensed something was odd with what Tanner was about to do. She questioned him, "Aren't the manuscripts supposed to be with the Preserver of the Nine until we decide to reveal our work for the benefit of mankind?"

Tanner answered, "If they could kill Nivedita Kaur and send someone to kill me, then it means that the Preserver is also in danger. That is why I must take the manuscripts with me.

"Now don't ask me any more questions because I'm stressed about what just happened and I need to find those manuscripts before any other assassinator tries to kill me."

Ananya whispered into Leena Gokhale's ear, "I have noticed something off about Tanner. It seems suspicious that he is leaving us and taking the manuscripts with him." The very next second an argument was about to ignite its spark amongst all of them.

"Mark you can't just leave us and take the manuscripts with you. You'll be leaving us in the face of danger. You would clearly not be doing your job, which is to protect us," said Stefan in an attempt to stop Tanner from absconding with the old manuscripts.

Leena Gokhale added, "Besides, only the head of the Nine can approve of a non-member carrying any version of the manuscripts with them."

"Unfortunately Nivedita Kaur isn't here with us anymore. And to ensure that no one else gets their hand around these manuscripts, I will do whatever seems necessary and safe for them. Considering that I'm the Saviour of the Nine," argued Tanner.

"But Nivedita's Lieutenant is here. Besides, that Saviour title has been self-proclaimed by you and I do not trust you nor do I allow you to run away with these manuscripts," ordered Gokhale.

Tanner again, started explaining his decision, "The fact that they know that Kaur is the head of the Nine, the fact that they know our location and even sent someone to kill us, clear shows that there is someone on the inside who is leaking information about us. This is dangerous for these manuscripts which is why I am taking them with me! Try to understand folks!"

"The leak could also be by you Tanner. How do you expect us to trust you?" argued Shilpa Dixit.

"Come on, please! We have worked together for almost a decade, and I have protected you all this time. You need to trust me, and I promise I will contact you," Tanner used the emotional appeal in order to gain their trust. He added, "I will also share my location with all of you." Convinced by this, the Nine Unknown allowed him to take the older version of the manuscripts with him. "It's not me who is the mole, I promise!" he added in order to ensure that no suspicion is raised against him by the Remaining Eight.

Tanner was very scared, stressed, and anxious as some random guy had showed up today to kill him. He needed to run away to save his life and get those manuscripts in his hands. Dr. Gokhale frowned, looking at how Mark Tanner just left them presumably in the fatally dangerous situation. Assuming that this man who was attacked them today had come here to finish them off and is possibly the same man who murdered Nivedita Kaur.

* * *

The elevator doors opened on the lobby floor. Ishir walked towards the lobby pressing his hand on the area on his head that was hit by the blow given by Tanner. He walked towards the sitting area in the lobby where the Nine were reclining on lounging chairs with worried faces. He walked towards the area where the Nine were sitting, the noise of the heavy stomping black shoes made Tobey Fox turn around. Ishir said, "Don't worry. I promise I won't hurt you guys. I have no weapon on me and if you guys do not believe me then you can call the cops on me."

Dr. Dixit questioned, "How are you planning to explain yourself?"

"This British gentleman, your very own James Bond, is actually someone very fishy and I am looking for him for a reason."

Rupert Roy asked softly, "Why? What for?"

Ishir looked at his watch and asked, "Anyone hungry? It's time for dinner."

* * *

A long joint table was in the outdoor dining area of the Aristocrat's Hotel where the ten people were sitting and having dinner. All the eyes were focused on Ishir who was munching on his food, as he completed chewing the morsel in his mouth.

He sipped on to his glass of water and began, "Sorry, I did not introduce myself earlier. My name is Ishir Singh and I work for this mercenary group where I conduct unauthorised missions by government agencies to take down bad guys." Taking a pause, Ishir resumed after he looked around the table, "You guys have this guy working for you all named Mark Tanner. For me and for the guys paying me, he is an MI6 file under the category of rogues and fugitives. Seven years ago, Mark Tanner was being investigated under charges of corruption and bribery, and he was working with these bad bunch of people. For seven years the MI6 tried tracking him and made every single note of his movements. But he, being a pretty damn good agent, has always found a way to erase evidence and come clean. The people he worked with were these powerful people like billionaires and scientists who had high-level connections. Which is why the MI6 paid me to find Mark Tanner, take him down along with these bunch of people he works with."

"Why are you telling us this information? We are just civilians," questioned Ananya. Inquiring if this man named Ishir knew about the possible existence of the Nine Unknown.

Ishir continued, "Because you are the Nine Unknown. My organisation, more or less my mercenary group does thorough research on you guys. The RAW'S Chief knows about you and so does the MI6. Mark Tanner was a high profile agent who had knowledge about this. The MI6 director did not know that his real intentions, so he assigned him to protect you guys under an unofficial order. Later, we found some evidence on him. He was working for these bunch of people called the Sword Of Power lead by this man who mints money and would wipe out any evidence, just like dust that flies from a child's blow."

Dr. Dixit asked, "What do you think are Mark's intentions?"

Ishir answered, "He works for the Sword Of Power in the dark, undercover. On paper, he is working for you guys with the title of *"The Saviour"* of the Nine but he plans to kill all of you. Steal your works, share it with the Sword of Power for the raining cash that he will be rewarded with. He doesn't care about what happens to the world because destruction will happen inevitably."

Ananya added on, "The very fear of Ashoka when he formed the Nine Unknown. He implied that if these nine manuscripts get into the wrong hands then it could cause complete destruction."

Ishir implied, "We must stop them at any cost. Your research formed with all your hard work, sweat, and blood, catalysing in a catastrophe will be a nightmare."

# CHAPTER-15

**9:30 p.m.**

**Room 1086**

**Aristocrat's Hotel**

**Delhi**

Ten people arrived inside Mark Tanner's room. The hotel staff was helpful with opening Mark Tanner's suite with a master key usually kept for emergencies. All the ten people were seated on the chairs, coffee table and the bed of Mark Tanner's suite.

Ishir wondered and asked, "Why was Nivedita Kaur killed?"

"Because she was the head of the Nine. The oldest member," answered Dr. Gokhale.

Ananya wondered, "Isn't Mr. Rupert the eldest member of this society?"

Dr. Gokhale explained, "He may be the eldest but Dr. Kaur has been a part of this society longer than any of us. Eldest member does not necessarily mean the oldest."

Ishir thought out loud, "Did Nivedita Kaur have any responsibilities as head of the Nine?"

Rupert Roy said, "Every head of the Nine has a specific key. Only two individuals possess this key. The head of the Nine and the Preserver of the Nine. This specific key opens up a big chest called the Ashoka's chest. That's all we know." Rupert took a pause to continue what he instantly remembered, "Not to forget that once the head of the Nine opens the chest then nine heavy books are revealed and each member of a specific subject has a specific key which is used to open the manuscript."

Ananya was amazed by such a advanced and smart way of securing a manuscript, rather a group of manuscripts. She was curious about how various subjects such as Sociology, Cosmology, Light, Communication, Gravity, Alchemy, Microbiology, Propaganda, and Physiology could be used for the development and progress or could lead to massive destruction. Considering that Ishir proved that Mark Tanner was a possible threat for the Nine and for RAW, as well as MI6, she felt that there was a high chance of Tanner misusing the information for money.

Ananya asked, "What is the use of the nine subjects which can create a positive or negative impact on the world?"

Dr. Isaac Joseph warned, "The knowledge in these manuscripts are much beyond the human capabilities of understanding and fathoming. No layman can understand it. Only an expert of a field can understand and use it. Either in a positive or in a negative way."

Ananya questioned, "Then how do you use the concept of gravity, Dr. Joseph? Considering that is your subject of expertise."

Dr. Isaac Joseph explained about the use of gravity, "I study and update information about gravity as work on building anti-gravity spaceships. The various *vimanas* in the ancient texts such as the Ramayana and the Puranas are an example of ancient inventions. Raavana's Pushpak vimana is an example of how an anti-gravity spaceship could be built. NASA built its spaceships based on the designs inspired by the Pushpak vimana."

Ananya interrupted, "Didn't Newton discover gravity approximately 400 years ago? And I'm assuming that Ashoka formed this secret society more than 2000 years ago. So how did gravity become a subject of study?"

Dr. Isaac corrected Ananya, "Brahmagupta, an ancient Indian mathematician and astronomer claimed that bodies fall towards the Earth as it is in the nature of the Earth to attract bodies just as it is in the nature of water to flow. This was a statement that Brahmagupta claimed about gravity in the year 628 AD, which was much before Newton's discovery of gravity."

Ananya loved playing the devil's advocate just to formulate a strong point even if she was blindly in favour of it. She corrected Dr. Isaac, "You just mentioned 628 AD. While Ashoka died in 232 BCE! Could there be another way to prove that gravity was a subject of Ashoka's secret society at the time when he found it?"

Isaac waited patiently. He took a moment to pause to recollect and resumed, "As I mentioned, the Pushpak vimana can be considered as an evidence of anti-gravity. So we can assume that ancient Indians had knowledge about gravity during the Treta Yug, approximately between 7000 to 11000 years ago or even before that."

"What about communication?" inquired Ananya.

Tobey Fox, who was half-inebriated and half-sleepy after a heavy meal said, "There are two types of communications in the Manuscript of communication. There is terrestrial and extraterrestrial communication. There's also communication of code languages, verbal, and non-verbal communication. Communication using machines and robotics is what I research on. Not to forget that the manuscript also records communicating with animals and understanding animal languages and animal psychology. In fact, a French-Roman scholar named Sylvester who met this secret society, possessed a bronze doll which could answer close-ended questions in yes or no. This could probably be considered as the first AI doll ever. When Sylvester decided to spread this information to the world…he died a mysterious death. Which is why the post "Saviour of the Nine" exists. So, Mr. Roy was quite accurate about how this knowledge is quite ahead of today's time and it is very unfathomable to common people." Tobey resumed sipping his coffee which had now gone cold. The same cup of coffee in which Tanner poured some white-coloured powder.

Ananya wondered about Cosmology, "And how important is Cosmology to the Nine?"

Shilpa Dixit explained the role of Cosmology to the Nine, "The book of Cosmology records the exploration of the universe. The multiverses and parallel universes and the exploration of galaxies beyond the milky way. Something that is shown in the Marvel and Star Wars movies, and podcasters fervidly discuss about. The manuscript also talks about an exploration on the topic of the anti-gravity aircrafts and spaceships which could travel faster than the speed of light, bending the space–time continuum. As well as about manipulating the four dimensions: length, breadth, height, and time. Especially manipulating time!"

Ananya turned towards Dr. Leena Gokhale, "Then what about Alchemy, Dr. Gokhale?"

Dr. Gokhale answered, "The Manuscript of Alchemy consists of the transmutation of metals, how to smelt and create gold. Discovering ways of curing and causing diseases. The manuscript discovers ways of extending life-expectancy and anti-ageing. The Somras in the ancient texts talks about the entire idea of anti-ageing and extending one's life expectancy. Have you ever wondered how India has a lot of gold despite having just a handful of gold mines? It is mainly because of two reasons: global trade and alchemy. The manuscript also consists of recipes of various potions and elixirs, how to use them, how to brew them, and how to counter them as well. The manuscript of alchemy also explores the element of Mercury and antidotes against Mercury."

"Then what's the use of Propaganda, Mr. Roy?"

The old Rupert Roy was busy combing his hair with his fingers, when he heard his name. He scratched his white beard and began, "What I've written so far as a journalist and as the writer of the Propaganda manuscript: I have written about psychological warfare, spreading rumours, moulding mass opinion, and these petty online battles on Twitter and other social media platforms are basically a byproduct of Propaganda. As a teenager, I have written about a war and I have covered stories from the frontline with a gun and a camera in my hand. There are very few who are interested in understanding a war. Various wars through the years of the history across the globe have been recorded, and various successful strategies to dictate any kind of warfare through spreading propaganda and polarization can bring down an entire civilisation! This can enable anyone to govern the whole damn world just through the propagated political influence. If this power goes into the wrong hands, then any bloody bloke can cause havoc in this world!" panicked the old Englishman Rupert.

"Then why Physiology?" asked the highly inquisitive Ananya wanting to know more details about the secret society. While Ishir is a little sleepy, he is trying to keep his eyes awake to know more information which could help him in this mission.

Dr. Ashwin Tripathi explained the role of Physiology being a part of the nine manuscripts. "The manuscripts contain secret information on how to kill people just by a touch, many people call it the touch of death which entails reversing a person's nerve impulse. There are various techniques of killing people with bare hands and multiple ways of killing people through techniques to kill them in a split second. There are also antidotes and ways of healing people affected by touches of death. The manuscript also consists of the research about biohacking, genetic modification, genetic hacking, and genetic engineering of test tube babies. There are also such horrifying and disastrous methods that one can use if God forbid this manuscript falls in the wrong hands."

Ananya asked Dr. Paula Maxwell about the use of microbiology. "Microbiology is a subject of studying things too small to be seen by the naked eye. The Manuscript of Microbiology consists of developing bioweapons to create viruses and developing bioweapons to combat viruses, as well as biotechnology. The manuscript records how to sting and poison people and also a type of gel that helps in erasing evidence. There is also mention of finding the traces even if they have been erased. It is used by the police while investigating murders but this type of gel can also detect a virus that no microscope in this world could detect. And also what Dr. Tripathi mentioned about biohacking, genetic modification, gene manipulation, those topics are also recorded in the manuscript."

The intrigued Ananya raised her eyebrows as she got to know more about all the subjects. She wanted to inquire about light from the German light engineer Dr. Stefan Schmidt. Before she could ask about the Manuscript of light, she took a moment to realise that almost all of them were PhD doctorates except Rupert Roy and Tobey Fox. "The last one in this room, Dr. Schmidt?"

"Einstein once asked his teachers: what is light? They couldn't answer it and no one can still exactly answer the question of what is light? Except, the Manuscript of Light."

Ananya interrupted Schmidt, "One second Dr. Schmidt," she picked her phone and opened up Safari to search up the definition of light. "As per Britannica, light is the electromagnetic radiation that can be detected by the human eye."

"Well, Britannica is not wrong, I never said that. But even Einstein proved that light is not just an electromagnetic wave or an electromagnetic radiation. Einstein proposed that light was not a continuous wave but a strain of localised particles. Light consists of strenuous waves made of minute particles which consists of photons and matter like protons, electrons, and neutrons. The manuscript develops a much deeper explanation towards the vast concept of light, it's properties and whatnot. I'm sorry but it is something only a physicist could understand."

"Simplify it. Only an expert can simplify things," persisted Ananya.

"Well, the localised particles have an electromagnetic radiation which makes them visible with the human eye. What makes them visible is the photons travelling through the waves of electromagnetic radiation." Schmidt switches off the lights of the room and turns his phone's flashlight on. The room turns pitch dark and Schmidt's flashlight is the only source of light now. Schmidt continues his explanation, "You see there is a ray from my phone's flash, right? That ray is basically a strenuous wave of electromagnetic radiation consisting of photons. That is light!"

"The manuscript has deeper and much more complex answers about light. Including information about weapons with the help of light such as lasers, lightsabres et cetera. Rather, their advanced version, which no one should even try to explore. These are just examples of weapons shown to you in movies and video games. Like Star Wars."

Ananya didn't hesitate to continue arguing with Schmidt, "Well I haven't watched Star Wars, nor do I play any of those dumb, childish video games. But sure these weapons do sound cool and threatening."

"The subjects of cosmology, communication, and light have been integrated together and these three subjects and the members who study them have been deeply involved in the research of quantum computing. The quantum computer has such unbelievable potential and can process such deep knowledge that one can say in principle that it is most certainly, infinitely faster than today's computers," continued Schmidt.

"We started researching with quantum computing ever since Richard Feynman proposed the need of a quantum computer to understand quantum simulations. China and USA have started working on this very recently while we have been researching on it much before they did," added Shilpa.

Ananya took a moment to realise one thing and decided to think it out loud, "Why did Mark take a bunch of briefcases from you guys?"

# CHAPTER 16

**The Sword Of Power Mansion**
**Hampshire**
**London**

All members of the Sword of Power had gathered up at their mansion at Hampshire, London, which was on the outskirts of London, far away from the daily hustle-bustle and stuffed studios inside Georgian style old buildings. This lavish yet old and huge mansion consisted of a large dining table, various bedrooms, study rooms, a huge library with colossal bookshelves touching the ceiling, and a conference room which was the same size of a ballroom where the Sword of Power often had their meetings.

The Sword of Power was another secret society established to liquidate all members of the Nine Unknown and steal all their manuscripts. These manuscripts would be studied by the members who were experts of specific fields who would eventually use them for their personal benefit.

Rather, misuse them. All members of the Sword of Power were college professors of subjects like Cosmology, Light, Alchemy, Microbiology, Physiology, and Gravity. Subjects like Sociology, Propaganda, and Communication were assumed to be easily understandable as they are social sciences by Richard Burton. However, they were underestimating the knowledge in the manuscripts.

Burton spent millions of dollars on establishing this society and paid an MI6 agent with codename, Orion with the sole job to liquidate all nine members and to steal all their manuscripts and hand them over to the Sword of Power. There were two members of the Nine who were on Burton's payroll. One was a veteran journalist and the other was an MI6 agent who was supposed to be the Saviour of the Nine. Someone whose job was to protect the Nine and provide safety and security. Especially from rival secret societies such as the Sword of Power. Clearly, the Saviour of the Nine was not doing his job efficiently as he went rogue ever since he joined the Nine in 2014, two years after the Sword of Power was established as a secret society.

Burton took a puff of his fat Cuban cigar and smoked it like a dragon. He took a sip of his expensive scotch and refilled it with twice the amount that he had just finished into his glass. He began, "Gentlemen, the first kill of the Nine Unknown has already happened. Once the manuscripts are in our hands, then our agent, Orion will kill all of them, and finally, we will take over the world!"

The Sword of Power's head, Richard Burton had all the money to pay them to shut up. Those who were forcefully working for the secret society such as Kenny Roman and Lalit Bakshi had been threatened. Burton's contacts with a high-profile surveillance agency kept an eye on all the members to ensure that they do not rebel. If they did, then they would be killed. An incident occurred a few years ago, where a member wanted to go against Burton by deciding to report it to a famous newspaper. Before she could contact the reporter, the surveillance agency killed her and buried her body under the very mansion Burton lives in. Not a single hint of evidence against him. A few years ago, Burton was accused of dealing weed and cannabis with a famous Cuban mafia with the use of dark web, considering that dark web has multiple layers of anonymity. Yet there was no evidence in spite of investigating all his devices. Burton sold the drugs from Cuba to high school students in London. Scotland Yard found very minimal and circumstantial evidence which forced the court to set him free and as innocent. Burton expected a call from Orion any minute now.

# CHAPTER 17

**Room 1086,**
**Aristocrat's Hotel,**
**Delhi**

Shilpa Dixit answered Ananya's question about the briefcases, "Those briefcases contain a manuscript and a box inside it containing a key. The manuscript is an older version that we have been working on and the key opens the actual book of all nine subjects."

"Where is the actual book?" asked Ananya.

"It is with the Saviour of the Nine," answered the cosmologist in her forties.

"And who is the saviour?" Ananya asked once again. Clearly, she had no hesitation asking multiple questions. But the Remaining Eight apparently weren't ready to disclose so much information.

Suddenly, Tobey started choking. His body felt dizzy and he collapsed like a tower made of Jenga blocks. His face turned a little blue, and white-coloured foam started spewing out of his throat. Tobey lost his breath, his pulse, and died. Ishir noticed Tobey drinking coffee from his styrofoam cup. Maybe that could have poisoned him. Ishir took a sniff of the styrofoam cup and felt a little dizzy. The foam created from his saliva and the aftereffects that he noticed on Tobey's body made him assume that Tobey must have died of cyanide poisoning. To confirm, Ishir decided to investigate the entire room. Everyone in the room was shocked and confused about Tobey's sudden death. Ishir looked under the bed and found a vial that resembled to powdered sugar. He picked it and announced "Cyanide, looks a lot like powdered sugar. Maybe that is what Mark added to Tobey's coffee, since this is Mark's room. It means that the Nine Unknown are under danger."

Ishir lifted Tobey's corpse. Dr. Leena Gokhale grabbed a black box. Looking at Gokhale, Ananya too donned her backpack to her shoulders as she had some important notes and documents with her, including the black box her Sociology professor gave her, and rushed out of Tanner's suite as Rupert grabbed the room key and held the door open for her on their way out to the nearby hospital. Out of the nine members of the secret society, there were only seven left to survive.

# CHAPTER 18

**High-Hat Regency**
**South Delhi**
**Delhi**

Mark Tanner, the rogue Saviour of the Nine escaped to a hotel closer to the Delhi Airport. As he checked in, he noticed a bunch of teenagers wearing formal attire such as suits and formal skirts. He later observed and realised that they are all participating in an MUN after glancing at their ID badges hung by a thick-ribboned sling.

Tanner checked inside his hotel room. He placed all nine briefcases on the bed. Then, he removed his shirt and walked inside the bathroom wearing his white tank top to freshen up. His stubble beard slowly growing on his face made him decide to shave. Not really a fan of stubbles or beards, he decided to splash some water on his face. He applied shaving cream on his neck, then his chin, after that he lathered his cheeks with the shaving cream releasing a mix of a floral and woody scent, and finally applied on his upper lip too. As he was done creating his white and cloudy beard made of shaving cream, Mark rinsed his shiny-bladed razor from the hotel room's shaving kit placed on the corner of the basin's slab. He cleaned up his cloudy cream beard and smoothly removed all stubble patches of beard growing on his face.

As Mark was about to finish shaving, a bit of aggressive hand near the chin caused a slight cut on the left side of his chin reaching his jawline. After shaving, he decided to apply some aftershave lotion on his face, especially his chin where the blood from the razor's cut was still dripping onto the basin. The aftershave lotion caused some stings on his entire face. He splashed some water on his face and washed his face. As his long hair were falling on his face, he combed it to slick the falling hair parting it on the crown of his head. He gently wiped his face with a Turkish towel and walked out of the bathroom. Then, he grabbed one of the briefcases, resting it on the coffee table of the hotel room. He sat on the yellow chair with his phone and a briefcase on the table. He placed his spectacles on his nose. He was in his early fifties, he maintained his body well enough to look like a man in his forties, but his eyes were of a fifty year old.

He unlocked his phone and opened Notes app where he had written all numeric codes for each briefcase. Clearly, his memory took a fall from twenty years ago when he had the capacity to remember everything during all his covert operations where it was all about information, stealth, deception, and memory. The four components of a spy.

He grabbed a briefcase at random called the Pataliputra briefcase. The numerical lock could be scrolled like the scroll wheel of a mouse. There were three such scroll wheels and the secured briefcase's code digit was supposed to be unlocked from the top. Each digit moving to the right is in an ascending order. He scrolled the digits for the lock's code to show 2-3-2. Each lock's code had a significant meaning behind it. 232 was the year when Ashoka died in Pataliputra. He opened the briefcase and found the old Manuscript of Propaganda and black coloured box with the Ashokan seal in the middle of the cover's lid.

Tanner put the briefcase on the floor called the Rinpoche briefcase and carefully placed the past manuscript and black-coloured cuboid box with Ashoka's seal beside it. He opened his phone and scrolled the next briefcase's lock to the digits 2-5-0. Which is supposed to be considered as Ashoka's year of conversion to Buddhism at Sarnath under Guru Rinpoche. He opened the briefcase and gently placed the same black-coloured cuboid box and the past Manuscript of Communication carefully on the table and the briefcase on the floor.

Tanner opened the third briefcase called the Buddha briefcase and scrolled through the digits of 108, a significant number in Hindu and Buddhist spirituality with multiple scientific, historical, and spiritual significances. There are 108 images of Lord Buddha around Kathmandu in Nepal, as well as the 108 desires and delusions an individual has in

Buddhism before attaining Nirvana. There could possibly be 108 meanings of the significant number 108. But the significance of 108 in Buddhism and Hinduism is high and it is code to open another briefcase of black box and the past Manuscript of Light.

Tanner grabbed the fourth briefcase called the Refuge briefcase. He scrolled through the digits to land up on the three digits 8-8-8. The three refuges in Buddhism were the sentences: Buddham sharanam gachchami. Sangham sharanam gachchami. Dhammam sharanam gachchami. Each of these lines had exactly eight syllables translated to: I take refuge in the Buddha, I take refuge in the *Sangha,* I take refuge in the Dharma. Hence the number 8-8-8. Which opened the Manuscript of Sociology. However, Tanner failed to find a black box in this briefcase. He did not ever remember opening it from when he killed Professor Nivedita Kaur to the time he checked inside the hotel and to the time he drove from Aristocrat's Hotel to Hyatt Regency. He was shocked, but he had to move to the fifth briefcase to see if it has the black box or not.

Tanner opened the fifth briefcase called the Ashoka briefcase and scrolled the digits to 3-0-4. The number 304 was the year of Ashoka's birth dating back to 304 BCE. Tanner was relieved when he opened the briefcase. He found the black box and the Manuscript of Cosmology. He hoped that there were no other briefcases that did not have the box. Tanner moved on to the sixth briefcase. He checked the Notes app on his phone to see how many are left. He pressed a tick emoji after every code of the briefcases marking it to be done. He threw the briefcase and repeated the same drill of placing the Manuscript of Cosmology carefully on top of the Manuscript of Sociology and carefully placed the black box on top of yet another black box.

Tanner grabbed the sixth briefcase called the Chandragupta briefcase and scrolled the digits to 3-4-0. The number 340 is connected to the birth year of King Ashoka's grandfather and founder of the Mauryan dynasty: Chandragupta Maurya who was born in the year 340 BCE, thirty six years before Ashoka was born. Tanner removed the Manuscript of Gravity and repeated the drill.

Tanner grabbed the seventh briefcase called the Chanakya briefcase and scrolled through the digits 3-7-5. The number 375 is connected to the birth year of the Prime Minister of the Mauryan empire, the great strategist and author of the Arthashastra and Chanakyaneeti. The great strategist Chanakya, also known as Vishnugupt and Kautilya. Western historians see Chanakya as the Indian Machiavelli. However, Chanakya lived centuries before the Italian diplomat and writer Niccolo Machiavelli, hence Machiavelli could be considered as the Italian Chanakya. Chanakya was an important part of the Mauryan empire. With his assistance and guidance to Chandragupta Maurya, the Mauryan empire was established and prospered because of the tactical and calculative strategies of Chanakya. A genius kingmaker who overthrew the arrogant and ignorant king Dhana Nanda, the last heir of the Nanda dynasty. He had insulted Chanakya in his courthouse, after which Chanakya vowed revenge and finally overthrew Dhana Nanda. Tanner kept the manuscript aside.

Tanner grabbed the eight briefcase called the Bindusara briefcase and scrolled through the digits 3-2-0. Which is connected to the year 320 BCE which is the birth year of Ashoka's father and predecessor Bindusara, who was the second king of the Mauryan dynasty. Tanner found the black box and the Manuscript of Physiology. He placed the black box and the old manuscript on top of the two huge piles. Tanner spoke to himself in his British accent, "Phew! Finally! One last briefcase to go."

Tanner grabbed the ninth and the last briefcase called the Kalinga briefcase, he scrolled through the digits 3-6-1, which is linked to the year 361 BCE. The year when the Kalinga war was fought. The war which ended it all, the war which broke Ashoka the King, and the war which made Ashoka convert to Buddhism. The very war of Kalinga which became the root cause of forming this secret society called, "The Nine Unknown" who would work on various subjects and preserve knowledge to use it to prevent similar or much worse events like Kalinga. He opened the briefcase and placed the old Manuscript of Alchemy on top of the Manuscript of Physiology. The brown-leathered covers of the manuscripts sitting on top of each other clearly resemble all fifty-four Jenga blocks horizontally resting on top of one another, waiting to eventually fall. The same case was with the boxes. A slight push would make all manuscripts or boxes tumble and fall on the ground. Tanner did not find a black box for the Kalinga briefcase either. He was anxious about where could the two keys from the Refuge and the Kalinga briefcases go? He was freaking out and getting jolts from imagining what could happen if he did not find them. Tanner took his phone and called up a contact number saved as the name "Purret".

# CHAPTER 19

**10:30 p.m.**
**A Nearby Hospital**

"I need to tell you something about Ashoka's secret," revealed the grey-haired Gokhale as the steam from the filter-coffee in a small paper cup was clouding the frames of her spectacles. Ananya, Dr. Gokhale, Shilpa Dixit, and Paula Maxwell were sitting in the hospital's canteen downstairs, drinking tea and coffee in paper cups.

Tobey had been admitted to a hospital closer to the hotel. They were all waiting for Tobey's autopsy and were reluctant to tell his family. His family included his two children who were living with his ex-girlfriend and his uncle living in Massachusetts who hadn't contacted him in years. Only his uncle's son was in touch with him from time to time, Tobey's cousin Max Fox.

Rupert, Dr. Ashwin Tripathi, Schmidt, and Isaac Joseph were sitting in the corridor of the autopsy room. They were waiting for the body to get transferred into the morgue, after which they were planning to leave. Rupert received a call from Mark and headed downstairs to answer it in the lawn. As he walked down the lobby's stairs towards the small lawn of the hospital, he answered the call. Ananya moved her eyes towards Rupert who was on his phone, smoking a cigar as he was speaking to Mark. "Yes Mark? What now?"

The anxious Mark said, "I can't find the bloody keys from the Kalinga and Refuge briefcases. Does anyone from the Nine have them?"

A surprised Rupert raised his right eyebrow, "The Kalinga and Refuge briefcases were for Sociology and Microbiology right?"

"Yeah! I remember the briefcase had been locked the night I came to kill Kaur. Bloody hell!" recalled the frustrated Tanner.

"What if someone in the Nine has them?" wondered Rupert.

"Ask around, especially Kaur's Lieutenant Gokhale and call me back once you find something," instructed Tanner and hung up.

* * *

Dr. Gokhale, Shilpa Dixit, Paula Maxwell, and Ananya walked inside the elevator heading upstairs towards the terrace of the building. By the time Rupert reached the elevator, the four of them had already stepped inside the lift which was heading to the terrace. Ishir followed Rupert to see where was he going as he overheard Rupert saying something suspicious about briefcases.

Dr. Gokhale, Paula, Dr. Dixit, and Ananya reached the terrace. That is when Gokhale resumed her conversation. "The Ashoka's Secret is a chest that contains all nine manuscripts. This chest can only be opened by two individuals when the information in the manuscripts is to be revealed to the world. The first one was the head of The Nine: Dr. Nivedita Kaur, the second one is the Preserver of the Nine."

"Who is the Preserver of The Nine?" asked Ananya.

"The head of The Nine is dead. But the head of the Nine always appoints a Lieutenant inside the Nine, the Lieutenant of the Nine appoints a Second Lieutenant and the Second Lieutenant appoints a Third Lieutenant and so on and so forth. So clearly in situations like these, there is an active chain of command or a line of succession to not mess this up. Since Nivedita appointed me as her Lieutenant. It shall be me."

"How is Ashoka's chest opened?"

"The Ashoka's chest contains a key to open the chest. Once you insert the key, you have to answer three questions on a screen. If you get them right then you open the manuscripts. Each manuscript has a designated key for each subject in our briefcases."

"The briefcases that Tanner stole from us," reminded Ananya.

Gokhale smiled and opened her jacket's pocket. She removed a black cuboid box with the Ashokan emblem. She slowly opened the lid and showed a key resting inside the box. Paula helped Dr. Gokhale by holding the lid. Gokhale showed the key to her. It was a golden primary style key with four Ashokan lions and the subject 'Microbiology' written as 𑀚𑀻𑀯𑀰𑀸𑀲𑁆𑀢𑁆𑀭. Ananya unzipped her pistachio-green coloured backpack and removed the similar black box as shown by Gokhale. She removed her key which was the replica of Gokhale's key, the same golden primary styled key with Ashoka's four lions on the back of the key as the key's handle with Sociology written in Brahmi as 𑀲𑀫𑀸𑀚𑀲𑁆𑀢𑁆𑀭, which is translated from the Roman Harvard–Kyoto method to Brahmi to translate and study Indian scripts such as Devanagari, Brahmi, and Pali.

Rupert was peeping through the door of the terrace that was left half-open. He saw the keys being shown by Ananya and Gokhale. Ishir who was just a few steps away from Rupert stood silent and did not move an inch of his muscle. Ishir quickly pointed his pistol towards Rupert in a fraction of a second, urging himself to take a shot but wanted to catch the bigger fish Mark Tanner. That is what his assignment from RAW was meant for—to catch and kill Mark Tanner unofficially. Rupert sensed that Ishir was following him so he decided to walk inside the terrace under the clear dark blue sky. He said, "I saw you guys coming upstairs so I decided to follow. What's up?" asked the old Brit as he limped inside the terrace. He noticed the key and asked, "Is that the key?"

"Yes, I kept mine and Kaur gave her the Refuge briefcase key. Probably Kaur knew that something like this was going to happen. I discreetly removed my key without anyone noticing back when Mark randomly asked us to hand over our briefcases."

Rupert tried not to act surprised, he smiled and said, "Smart move Leena!" and walked away with his limping left ankle which was losing bone density because of his age. As he walked downstairs, Ishir looked at him walking down and was observing each step of his movement still suspicious about what he heard him saying about the briefcases. Why did he mention the briefcases to someone? Who could it be? Mark Tanner?

Rupert dialled Tanner and informed him, "Mark! Kaur's Lieutenant, Gokhale has her key. She must have removed it when you asked everyone about the briefcases. She would have been suspicious about what you were doing or going to do when you asked for the briefcases, left us alone and ran away!"

Tanner smiled and sighed out of relief and said, "I'm on my way. Send me the location of the hospital and I'll get there as soon as I can." Tanner rushed out of his hotel room, he grabbed his key and ran towards the elevator at lightning speed. He punched the elevator's lobby button 3-4 times. As soon as the elevator landed on the ground floor. Tanner sprinted across the lobby of the hotel. As the valet got his car from the parking lot, Tanner jumped inside the car and started it. He clicked on the link that was sent by Rupert about his location and drove his car at lightning speed. Each time his car was accelerating, the sound of engines would be revving. The hospital was far away from the hotel that he was residing in, so he had to make it quick. As quick as possible to the hospital otherwise he would lose his chance of getting those two keys!

* * *

Ishir was on a call with the Chief of RAW, Suraj Khanna. RAW's Chief Khanna was the typical spy stereotype that was shown in the Bond movies. The sharp eyes, the charming smile, and the slick back hairstyle. He donned a suit and wore shades at all times while heading out. The typical debonair Bond image for RAW was their chief Suraj Khanna who worked in Istanbul and London. "Yes Suraj, what is the update?" asked the Chief as he touched his gelled hair and groomed it backwards with his fingers. "Sir it is certain that Orion is in Delhi. It is also clear that apart from the other eight charges that are accused on Orion, there is another one. And that is to murder the Nine Unknown, steal their manuscripts, and give them to the Sword of Power."

"So our surveillance on Tanner proved that the Nine do exist after all and that this was not a myth. Ishir, your job is not only to kill Tanner come what may but also to save the Nine. Keep them safe! This secret society is actually working for the good and sometimes, keeping all knowledge secret is also advantageous."

"I promise sir."

"Remember that this assignment about Mark Tanner is completely off the books. Yes, you are on RAW's and

MI6's payroll to kill Mark Tanner but you have to do that independently. MI6 has no idea that Tanner works for the Nine Unknown. They only know that he is in India for most of the time having meeting these scientists, professors and stuff. So your job is to guard the Nine as well. That is not the job of your organisation, the Wolf's Claw. It is yours."

"Roger that sir," Ishir assured.

* * *

Tanner reached the hospital; he removed a small 9 mm Glock 17 Beretta and turned the safety lock off. He checked the number of bullets and pulled the slide to see if the gun is loaded or not. He checked the magazine inside the pistol to check the number of bullets. He holstered his small black 9 mm Glock 17 Beretta to a black leather holster velcroid to his angle and covered it with his grey trouser. Tanner got out from his black SUV and walked inside the staircase of the hospital. He connected his phone to his Bluetooth earpiece and called Rupert. Rupert answered and instructed him, "Come upstairs to the topmost floor." Rupert got up from his seat at the hospital corridor and tried to walk on the staircase to reach the terrace.

Ishir saw Mark walk on the staircase and about to get inside the elevator. He sprinted from the hospital's lawn to the elevator like a cheetah. As soon as he made it to the elevator, Mark had already pressed the button to the topmost floor. Ishir hopped on to the staircase opposite to the elevator and ran as fast as he could to do his best to stop Tanner. As

Ishir galloped on the staircase going upwards he saw the elevator stopping on the third floor. He looked for the floor number he was on, which turned out to be the one above the elevator currently. The elevator had stopped as a doctor had pressed the button for the fourth floor. Ishir instantly pressed the button for the fourth floor, then he ran towards the fifth floor and pressed the button for the fifth floor, then the sixth, after that the seventh and finally the eight. After Ishir reached the ninth floor he took a pause to breathe and dialled Ananya to run away from the terrace because Tanner is coming to kill them. Ananya took Leena, Paula, and Shilpa down the staircase with a pace as fast as they could move to on their way to the staircase downstairs. Ishir led Isaac, Schmidt, Rupert and Ashwin downstairs as they all ran to the lobby.

The irritated Tanner finally made it to the terrace but as he reached the terrace he felt shameful of himself. A former MI6 agent couldn't realise that constantly stopping the elevators was another way of preventing him from killing Leena and Ananya to take the keys from them. Tanner galloped down the staircase till he found the elevator on the tenth floor and pushed the button for ten seconds rather than pressing it only once. The anxiety of losing the opportunity to grab the two missing keys reminded him to take out his gun from his ankle holster. As soon as the elevator doors opened, Tanner walked out of the lobby down the staircase and saw Ishir with the Remaining Seven get into an SUV. Dr. Gokhale was right behind Rupert holding the key in one hand and her purse in the other. Ishir noticed Tanner aiming at Dr. Gokhale, he was about to press the trigger to shoot her. Without giving a second to think, Ishir immediately pushed Dr. Gokhale who fell on her back on the ground as soon as Tanner pressed the trigger. The bullet hit Rupert's skull who died instantly. Ishir grabbed Rupert's phone, then lifted Dr. Gokhale quickly to make her sit inside the car. After that, Ishir jumped inside the driver's seat and started his car. Tanner ran closer towards Ishir's SUV and fired another bullet which hit the skull of Isaac Joseph. Along with Rupert, Dr. Isaac Joseph was also dead.

There were only five members from the Nine Unknown still surviving. The Remaining Five are in total shock and panic as they have noticed four deaths in this one day which has been more than enough trauma for them. First was the head of the Nine and Sociologist, Nivedita Kaur. The Second was the journalist working on the Manuscript of Communication, Tobey Fox. Third was the veteran journalist who wrote the Manuscript of Propaganda, Rupert Roy. Fourth was the Gravitational Physicist, Isaac Joseph.

# CHAPTER 20

**11:00 p.m.**
**Tanner's Suite**
**Room 1086**

The Remaining Five along with Ananya and Ishir walked inside Tanner's abandoned suite. Paula argued and questioned Ishir as he placed the key card inside the key holder. "Why did you throw Isaac's body out of the car? And why did you leave Rupert? What the hell is wrong with you? Are you also trying to kill us?"

"Paula you need to calm down! I can understand that you are in shock and panic. How the hell do you think Tanner could find us here? That is because I overheard a conversation between Rupert and someone, and who was that someone? Tanner! He is the one who came to kill us! And Rupert snitched on us. As far as Isaac is concerned, I'm sure that someone would have saved him given that he was thrown out near a hospital."

Ishir opened Rupert's phone with a pin. He asked the Remaining Five, "When is Rupert Roy's birthday?" Dr. Ashwin Tripathi answered, "16th March." Ishir attempted to crack Rupert's security pin on his phone by typing 1603 on the screen. The guess was correct; the screen unlocked and he was able to access Rupert's phone. Ishir was amazed by how he could easily crack Rupert's phone and gave a slight smile flashing a dimple. He opened the call logs on the bottom left of his phone and saw the recent call logs with a contact number saved as Mark Tanner. He showed it to the Remaining Five and asked rhetorically, "You want more evidence? Happy?"

Shilpa Dixit said, "Fine we believe you. But what now?"

Ishir took a moment to think. Ananya remembered something and asked, "What about the key that opens Ashoka's Secret?"

"There is a map through which one can open the chest. Ideally, there is only one person who can open it and who possesses a spare key to Ashoka's Secret."

"And who is that?" Ishir asked.

Leena said, "There is a map showing a way to find Ashoka's Key to Ashoka's Secret. There are three keys. The third one is with the Preserver, the one directed with the help of a map. Nivedita couriered the map to my house about two days ago because the head of the Nine is supposed to be in possession of the map. So I am assuming that Tanner has the map since he murdered Kaur."

"Then what about Ashoka's third key?" asked Ananya.

"There is one with the Preserver and there is one key that can be found with the help of the map that Tanner stole. The key is opened only through three symbols and is opened once every decade to preserve the re-written and updated manuscripts inside Ashoka's Secret."

"So Professor Kaur followed that trail through this map every ten years? In spite of walking with the help of a stick?" asked Ananya.

"Who said that the head of the Nine was supposed to do that? The head could often choose someone who could travel to store all the manuscripts through that map."

"And who was it?" asked Ishir.

Dr. Gokhale looked towards Dr. Ashwin Tripathi and answered, "Ashwin."

Ishir instructed, "Alright, Dr. Tripathi will help me and Ananya with the quest of the map. The Remaining Four will go to the Preserver."

Ananya stopped Ishir and asked, "Where does the Preserver live?"

Leena looked around and said, "'We need to go to Gaya."

# CHAPTER 21

**11:30 p.m.**
**High Hat Regency**
**South Delhi**
**Delhi**

Tanner reached his hotel and searched for his bag. He forgot that his bag was inside his suite at the Aristocrat's Hotel. A well-organised plan went for a toss, is what he told himself. All because of that one person who is after his life, and who is sabotaging the plan decided by the Sword of Power and himself. He remembered which bag had the wooden box. He opened his suitcase and to his relief, he found a wooden box with a cryptex. This was a three letter cryptex in the English language as compared to the Nine briefcases which were cryptexed in the Brahmi script.

For all these years that Mark served for the Nine, he was aware of this box and what it contained. He decided to do the obvious. He decided to enter the letters leading to a word, which is an object that is placed inside the box. For the first letter on the cryptex, Tanner scrolled to the letter M. For the second letter, he scrolled to the letter A. And for the third letter on the cryptex, Tanner scrolled to the letter P.

As Tanner slowly and carefully opened the box, he found three pieces of paper. They were three old maps on old, dated, and dusty pieces of paper. Tanner opened the maps one after the other. The first map was at the location of Ashoka Stambh in Delhi, previously known as Indraprastha during the Ashokan reign. The second map was of the location of Sarnath at Varanasi, what was called as Kashi during the Ashokan reign. And the third map was of the location of a cave at Patna in the state of Bihar, also called Pataliputra during King Ashoka's reign. Tanner walked out of his hotel room and followed the map of Delhi. He searched up Feroz Shah Kotla on the GPS and drove off from his hotel to the famous historical location at 11:30 p.m. in the night. Hopefully, Tanner would be able to find the first symbol without much crowd present.

Feroz Shah Kotla was one of the oldest structures in Delhi. A fort built in the year 1635 by the Delhi Sultan, Feroz Shah Tughlaq. This fort was built when Emperor Feroz Shah Tughlaq decided to shift his capital from Tughlaqabad to Firozanad due to the rising droughts and water scarcity. Which is why the fort called Feroz Shah Kotla was built on the banks of the Yamuna river.

The pristine sandstone Topra Ashokan pillar rises from the palace's crumbling remains. Ashoka's Topra pillar that was erected in Topra Kalan, in Pong Ghati of Yamunanagar district was moved from Haryana to Delhi and re-erected it in 1356 under Tughlaq's orders. The original inscription on the obelisk is primarily in Brahmi script but language was Prakrit, with some Pali and Sanskrit added later. The inscription was successfully translated in by an English scholar, orientalist, and antiquary—James Prinsep in 1837. Other than the Ashokan Pillar, the Fort complex also houses the mosque Jami Masjid—a reservoir also known as *Baoli* of King Agrasen, along with a large garden complex.

Tanner finally reached Feroz Shah Kotla. That entire neighbourhood consists of historical monuments. On one hand is the fortress of Feroz Shah Kotla, where is the Jami Masjid and the Topra Pillar. About a few hundred meters away is the Raj Ghat, a memorial dedicated to the freedom fighter who stood for non-violence: Mohandas Karamchand Gandhi, and another few hundred meters away is the Arun Jaitley Stadium (formerly known as Feroz Shah Kotla Stadium) dedicated to the former Finance Minister of India and former President of the Delhi Cricket Association.

It was extremely cold and hazy in the night. The winters of November in Delhi did not have much of an impact to Tanner as he was used to the similar weather temperature back home, in London. As Tanner walked out of his car, he saw a padlock attached to the latch of the black iron-barred grille door. He walked back to his car and opened the glove box in the front seat by pressing a button. After the glove box opened, Tanner removed a silencer. Tanner inserted the silencer on the muzzle of the gun and rolled it inside till it firmly fits the mouth of the muzzle. Once the silencer had settled in, Tanner pointed the gun at the padlock and whispers, "Fire in the hole," which is a phrase used by American miners while using dynamite to explode rocks in mines, later even used in the action movies of Hollywood. This Hollywood phrase was Tanner's favourite. He used it every time he would engage in a duel involving guns.

The bullet broke the padlock which fell from the latch. Tanner unlocked the latch of the iron grille door and sneaked inside Feroz Shah Kotla exactly at the moment when his watch made a sound indicating that it is midnight and a new day had begun. Tanner looked at his watch which showed the time 12:00 a.m.

Tanner ran towards the Pyramid of Cells on which Ashoka's Topra pillar rested. He jogged towards the staircase of the Pyramid of Cells and as soon as he climbed up the staircase, he noticed Ashoka's pillar with a bunch of Brahmi, Prakrit, and Pali inscriptions which did not mean anything to Tanner because he did not understand the three scripts. Tanner took another glance at the map

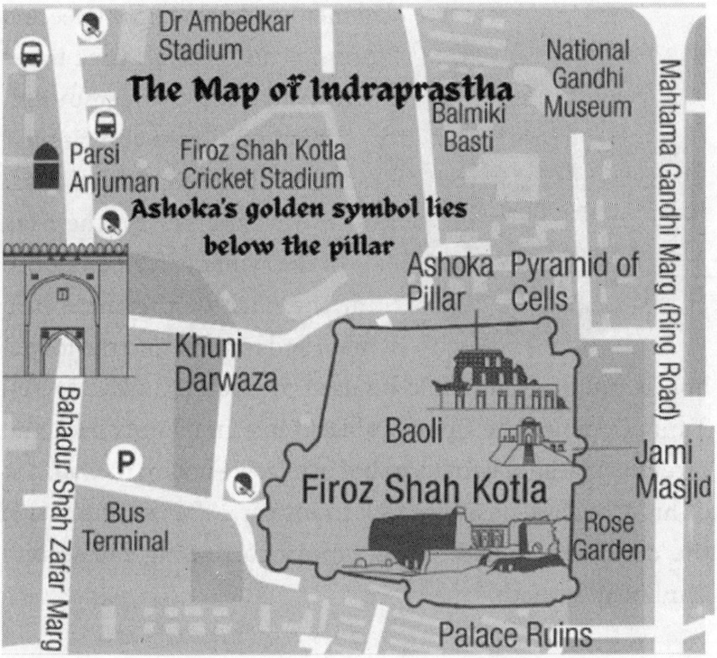


He had arrived at the exact spot where the pillar was located but he was not able to see anything. The map included a line written: *Ashoka's golden symbol lies below the pillar.* Tanner re-read that line and took his eyes away from the map. He looked at the entire surrounding where the pillar was located on the fortress in ruins made of granite stone and lime mortar. Tanner took another look at the map, and the moment he took his eyes away from the map, he noticed a shiny golden coloured symbol on the surface of the floor below the pillar. This shiny golden-coloured symbol made Tanner think, *What if this is Ashoka's first symbol?*

Tanner bended his right knee and pressed the symbol three times to find a way to remove it. The lions from the circular symbol slowly drifted apart to reveal a key on the back of the symbol. Tanner looked at the back of the three lion symbol and noticed that the fourth lion is the key that could be used to open Ashoka's secret. Tanner opened the zip of his black-coloured fanny pack and carefully placed the first symbol inside. He got up to walk out of his crouched position back to his car. After sitting inside the car, Tanner said, "Now I'm off to finding the second symbol at Sarnath."

# CHAPTER 22

**2:30 p.m.**
**The Sword of Power Safehouse**
**Hampshire**
**London**

Richard Burton, Kenny Roman, and Yao Zhi are the only three people present in the long and wide conference room of the Sword of Power. The big three of the secret society vowing to destroy the Nine Unknown and steal their manuscripts to take control of the entire world. The Sword of Power was basically anti-Nine Unknown. The three founders of the secret society were Richard Burton, Kenny Roman, and Yao Zhi.

Richard Burton, a billionaire with a deep voice similar to Sean Connery's James Bond, complimenting with a heavy British accent. His long, white, curly hair matching with his thick, white beard and his navy blue suit carrying a packet of Cuban cigars in his pocket, really made him look like a new James Bond villain. His brainchild—the Sword of Power was close to being successful, and within this week, he was expecting to have the nine manuscripts in his hands with the help of Mark Tanner. Burton was in the sky, daydreaming about the moment these manuscripts will be in his hands, and finally he could take control of the entire world. However, on the other hand, a part of his mind was diverted towards the anxiety of this decade-long plan going down the drain.

Kenny Roman was one of the founders who was also a news reporter, waiting to use the Manuscript of Propaganda. With a triangular face and gelled hair and stubble growing out, he walked inside the conference room and sat on a comfortable red Victorian chair as he came back from the evening news reading donned in a tan suit with a powder blue shirt and a bright red necktie. His reason for joining the nine is only that Richard Burton was his boss and is still his boss after joining the Sword of Power. Burton offered Kenny Roman to join the Nine Unknown, a fascinating offer for him who wanted to spread propaganda and instigate psychological warfare with the help of the manuscript written, researched, and studied by one of their own: the veteran British journalist Rupert Roy.

Yao Zhi was a physicist who was looking forward to studying the manuscripts of light, communication, and cosmology, was a Chinese scientist with well-established contacts with the CCP (Chinese Communist Party) and the MSS (Ministry of Security State; aka Chinese intelligence).

He joined this secret society with motives to hand over these manuscripts to the Chinese government, which is why he conducts virtual meetings with the head of the MSS through a Chinese virtual meeting platform and updates them regularly. At the end of this mission's success, Yao Zhi plans to kill all of them with the help of his connections with Chinese agents and flee to Beijing with the nine manuscripts and share them with the esteemed Chinese scientists, professors, bureaucrats, and defence officers.

The big three were awaiting to receive Mark Tanner's call from India any moment now. Burton's burner phone rang which he picked up instantly and answered, "Hey Orion, what is the status on the witch hunt?"

"You could call it more of a treasure hunt Hercules. I found a map from Kaur's possession; it would help me in finding the key."

Burton questioned, "Do you have a plan B? God forbid, If your treasure hunt fails?"

"Yes I do, I plan to steal the key from the Preserver of the Nine in case this treasure hunt doesn't work." Tanner continued, "Alright, so basically this map..."

Burton interrupted, "Orion, I don't care how you do it. I just want you to bring the Nine bloody manuscripts to the Sword of Power mansion."

"Orion, I would recommend sending a personal contact of mine who used to be in the MSS. An agent who can help us out with this. Like you...he too is a fugitive spy," suggested Yao Zhi.

"Well Mr. Zhi, I am capable of handling this on my own."

Yao stood adamant to his suggestion. "I would really recommend that you accept some assistance. He is not with the MSS anymore and he lives right here in London. He is the best in his work, and you two should work together if you want this mission to be successful."

Burton looked at Yao and whispered to the speakerphone, "It is an order Orion. I will have him fly down to Delhi before noon."

Tanner sighed out of frustration and agreed. "Fine! But have him reach here as soon as possible."

Burton hung up the call. A few minutes later, after a dozen puffs of his Cuban cigar, the remaining members of the Sword of Power walked in. Burton told them, "Gentlemen, our mission is about to come to an end. In a matter of a few days, we will rule this entire bloody world only with the help of these nine manuscripts and the knowledge that each word written in these books contain."

He looked at all members of the Sword of Power inside the mansion's conference room and continued his speech, "King Ashoka believed that knowledge is far more powerful than wealth, which is why he came up with this secret society. After a certain point, money is just a bunch of numbers on a piece of paper determining your financial assets. But knowledge, it is far more powerful and it determines a person's true intellect when he can use that knowledge in real life. All these bloody Ivy degrees won't determine your intellect unless you are greedy enough to chase knowledge.

A person with no money and vast knowledge can surpass a person with limitless money but with no knowledge. We are exploiting the leverage of Ashoka's secret society and his faith towards the path of knowledge. But if it allows us to control the world with such powerful knowledge, then why not?" laughed Burton as he asked the question rhetorically.

Burton spoke one last line before he ended his speech. "In chess, when the queen dies, that is the true demonstration of one's knowledge—to survive when your wealth and power is taken away from you. That is the exact central idea of the Sword of Power."

* * *

Yao Zhi was sitting on a chair waiting for someone in a typical European streetside cafe somewhere in Central London. As he noticed the double-decked London buses going by and watched packs of crowded people walking on and crossing the street. The person who he waited for finally came. A pudgy man in a leather jacket with pale skin and small eyes, with gelled slick back hair, sat on the chair in front of Yao Zhi. An MSS agent named Cheng Zhang greets Yao, "Ni hao Mr. Zhi."

Yao greets back saying, "Ni Hao Zhang." Yao begins the agenda of the conversation after the words of salutation have been exchanged. "I have a special assignment for you, something that will get you back in MSS."

"What is it?" asked Cheng as he sipped onto his green-coloured glass bottle of beer. Day drinking became a habit of

Cheng ever since he got fired from the MSS for conspiring against the Director of the MSS, to be a snitch. Day drinking for the past three years reflected onto his paunch.

"I need you to go to Delhi. You will meet our man named Mark Tanner. He is also a mole in an ancient secret society which possesses advanced knowledge that us Chinese can put into very good use. You bring those manuscripts to me and I promise you will be back on the force," Yao pulled out a ticket from his olive green blazer's breast pocket and placed it on the white table. "Your ticket to Delhi. Leaves in four hours. Go and pack your things now!"

"Well, it seems like I am going to India to end a war between secret societies," joked Cheng.

"Do you know the story of manuscripts in Tibet?"

# CHAPTER 23

**11:30 a.m.**
**Patna Airport**
**Bihar**

The Remaining Four have arrived in Bihar. The very origin of the Mauryan empire—in the state of Magadh, the capital of Pataliputra which is called Patna in today's day and time. After a heavy breakfast at the hotel, Ishir had dropped them to the airport which brings them to this state. They did not bring any luggage with them, since the briefcases were stolen by Tanner. Dr. Dixit and Dr. Gokhale live in Delhi, Dr. Isaac Joseph is in the hospital, Tobey Fox, and Rupert Roy were killed, leaving Dr. Paula Maxwell and Dr. Stefan Schmidt as the only members carrying their luggage which is inside their hotel rooms in Delhi. Meanwhile Ishir, Ashwin, and Ananya are yet to board their flight to a different destination.

Ishir, Ananya, and Dr. Ashwin Tripathi decided to take a different route to join the treasure hunt of Ashoka's key. After having a heavy breakfast with the other four, they decided to leave for Varanasi two hours later. Ananya's mint green leather bag contained some really important documents regarding her research related to Ashoka, which were a part of her research paper for her undergraduate course but now, these research documents might as well help her in this treasure hunt to find Ashoka's Key.

* * *

A huge black SUV arrived outside the airport's terminal in front of the Remaining Four. A man dressed in a black leather jacket, aviators, black jeans, and black formal shoes walked out of the car and said, "I am from the Wolf's Claw, Ishir told me to pick you outside this gate."

The Remaining Four sat inside the huge black SUV, the man dressed in an all-black ensemble drove off to an address texted by Ishir. This man named Eric put the address on his car screen's GPS and drove off to the location. About half an hour later, the SUV arrived in front of a Buddhist monastery atop a hill. Dr. Leena Gokhale got out of the car and takes a look around. As the Remaining Four reached the monastery by climbing up the slope, a message was sent out to one of the closest disciples of the Preserver saying, 'The Nine are here'.

The disciple of the Preserver led them to a quiet room where the Preserver was chanting the famous Buddhist mantra "Om Mani Padme Hum". As they walked inside the room, they saw a statue of a meditating Buddha with Om Mani Padme Hum written in the Tibetan script on the bottom of the lotus made of Greystone, standing behind the Preserver's back. They saw the Preserver meditating. The monk kept chanting the mantra "Om Mani Padme Hum" and moved a bead to the left completing one count, which he did repeatedly till he had reached the hundred and eighth bead.

The monk draped in a red and yellow Buddhist attire made of cotton opened his eyes. The Preserver of the Nine Unknown's manuscripts was a Tibetan monk named Rinpoche who arrived in the 1960s from a monastery in the icy mountains of Tibet. When he joined, he was a young Buddhist who was sent by the Rinpoche from a Tibetan monastery which was guarding the nine manuscripts. When Guru Rinpoche arrived in India, he approached the Nine Unknown through the monastery that he is the abbot of, which also guards the nine manuscripts inside Ashoka's Secret to this very day.

He slowly got up from his meditating mat and asked, "Why are all the Nine Unknown members not present here? Why just the four of you. Where is Dr. Kaur?"

"Your Holiness, we need to talk. In the library. The Nine Unknown are in danger."

The monk took his walking stick with him and opened a door to his chambers. The room consisted of a couch in front of the door's entrance and a desk on the other end of the chamber. Behind the desk is a wall of bookshelves. Rinpoche walked towards his desk with the help of his wooden stick and pressed a button on the bottom of his desk and said the line, “Om Mani Padme Hum.” Through voice recognition and finger recognition, his holiness had been able to enter the first two lines of security. The last line of security was a key that Dr. Gokhale possessed. She removed a small key from her pursue. It was the four lion Ashokan symbol which she placed inside one of the green covered books titled ‘Ashokvandana’.

Suddenly, one row of the bookshelf opened itself to be a part of a door through which the Remaining Four and the monk walked inside. Rinpoche pulled another book called The Nine Unknown by Talbot Mundy which helped in closing the bookshelf door. As soon as they walked inside the bookshelf, the Remaining Four and the Preserver walked down the staircase and found themselves to a black door. The black door was opened through a biometric recognition with the help of the Preserver and the head of the Nine. However, the head of the Nine had been murdered. But the Preserver opened the biometric shielded door in an alternative way, by rotating the statue of Buddha’s head placed on a side table to ninety degrees. Nobody knew that a spiritual teacher living in Gaya in his late seventies could be so fluent with technology. All members of the Nine Unknown including their Preserver knew how to use technology efficiently.

The Preserver of the Nine and the Remaining Four sat on their designated seats. Dr. Leena Gokhale began, “Nivedita Kaur, Tobey Fox, and Rupert Roy are dead. We are not sure about Isaac Joseph yet, but he is also in a critical condition.

Rupert Roy was the leak and so was Mark Tanner. We have reasons to believe that he killed all of them, starting with Kaur."

"Why?" asked the astonished Preserver.

Paula answered, "Tanner is on a secret society's payroll which is basically anti-Nine Unknown. He is helping them in killing us and stealing our researchwork."

"I can't even call for security because I will have to tell them the reason. What do I tell them? That there is a war between two secret societies and I am somehow affiliated with them?" said the Preserver.

Leena Gokhale said, "We have two people helping us, one is a student of Nivedita Kaur and the other is an agent. These two are trying to stop Tanner who is following the map of the Ashokan symbol, and Ashwin is assisting them with the map."

"All we can do is stay calm, pray to God, and hope for the best of these manuscripts," said the Rinpoche.

"What about your safety, Your Holiness?"

"I have had the great privilege to guard these manuscripts that possess immense knowledge for a long time. The safety of the nine manuscripts is paramount than me." The Preserver looked at the worried faces across the long table and said, "Destiny is the best writer."

# CHAPTER 24

**11:30 a.m.**
**Indira Gandhi International Airport**
**Palam**
**New Delhi**

Mark Tanner has checked inside the terminal of the Delhi Airport named after Indira Gandhi, India's first female Prime Minister. After walking past the security gate, Tanner walked in. However, the CISF officers along with governmental authorities were notified about a British agent named Mark Tanner of RAW. He is known for espionage related crimes against the Indian and British government related to money laundering, bribery, and the assassination of well-known scientists across the world. However, to the RAW chief, the allegations slammed on him are like euphemism for his real heinous crimes.

Cheng Zhang walked inside the food court with a picture of Mark Tanner in his phone. He was searching for Tanner and finally found him sitting inside a cafe, slowly sipping an espresso shot. Cheng looked at him and then looked at the image on his phone. He identified Mark Tanner and walked inside towards his table. Cheng whispers as he sits on the chair opposite of Tanner, "I'm the man Mr. Yao Zhi has sent."

"Ah! Finally, the man I was waiting for. Why did you agree to Yao? How do you know him?" asked Tanner as he took another sip of his espresso shot.

"I have been out of the force for so long. I needed an excuse to join back," replied Cheng as he thought of the actual reason in the back of his mind, which was to steal the manuscripts from Tanner, give them to Yao and eventually, hand them over to the Chinese experts to study these manuscripts.

"How do you know Yao is also my question."

"Mr. Zhi has several connections with the Chinese government and—"

"You mean your communist regime," interrupted Tanner.

Cheng did not appreciate the way Tanner interrupted him and his comment about his country. Even though it was true, Cheng's bitterness boiled and he continued, "Mr. Tanner, there are several charges on you, so you don't need to point fingers at my country pretending that your country loves you and is not chasing you for of the various crimes you have committed as an MI6 agent." He continued, "I read your file on the flight." Cheng resumed to answer Tanner's question, "And Mr. Yao has several connections with the CCP, the Chinese government, and Chinese agents."

"I read your file too Cheng. You were thrown off MSS for conspiring against your boss. So don't try to act like you are defending your country." Tanner was right about Cheng, but Cheng would obviously not reveal his plan to get back into MSS with the help of Yao Zhi, by stealing the original manuscripts from Tanner by the end of this mission. Tanner understood that he did the wrong thing by bad-mouthing Cheng's country. He decided to change the topic, so he pulled boarding passes from his off-white shirt's front pocket and put them on the table. He started a fresh conversation, "Our boarding passes, we leave in two hours to Varanasi."

* * *

Dr. Ashwin Tripathi, Ananya, and Ishir are sitting on one of the tables of the crowded food court of the Delhi airport. Ashwin begins, "We are on a treasure hunt to find the three golden-coloured symbols of the four lions. There are three symbols, one starting with the first symbol in Delhi, the second one is in Sarnath, and the third one is in Bihar. I am assuming that Tanner must have found the first one, but before he gets to the second and third symbol. We must stop him."

Ananya questioned, "How and why do you know so specifically about this map?"

Ashwin answered, "Before Nivedita Kaur, my father was the head of the Nine Unknown and this map was in his possession till the day he died. Then one day, I found out about this map and the Nine Unknown, and that is when Nivedita Kaur stepped up and asked me to join the Nine Unknown."

"Does your family know about this?" asked Ananya.

Ashwin digressed from the conversation, "Obviously not, we are supposed to hide it from our families. I found the map and everything else after my father died. So in case I die, God forbid my children have no idea about this because I had to follow my father's footsteps of Physiology."

"Why was I picked for this?" asked Ananya.

"Because you were trained for it," answered Ashwin, mysteriously.

Ishir looked at his watch from his military days and said, "Our flight leaves in an hour. Let's go."

* * *

"So why don't we use the past manuscripts?" asked Cheng as he sipped his iced coffee with a straw as he walked with Tanner towards the flight gates.

Mark explained, "These manuscripts are updated after each decade. If new information is discovered and the information inside the manuscripts lose their relevance then it is necessary to update it."

"When is the deadline of updating the next edition of the manuscripts?" asked Cheng as he took another sip of his iced coffee.

"Next year's *Buddha Purnima,*" answered Tanner.

Cheng asked, "What is that?"

"Buddha's birth anniversary."

* * *

Ishir, Ananya, Dr. Tripathi, Tanner, and Cheng were on the same flight. The plane took off to Varanasi airport. Mid-air, Ishir felt the urge to attend nature's call and walked towards the airplane's lavatory. The aisle seat of the middle row was occupied by an asleep Tanner. As soon as Ishir finished his nature's call and washed his hands. He saw Tanner and covered his face to walk towards his seat which was one of the seats at the very end of the plane, close to the plane's door. Ananya was in the middle while Dr. Tripathi was on the window seat. He tapped on Ananya's shoulder, she was busy trying to fall asleep with music playing in her earphones. With the jolt she received from Ishir tapping her shoulder, she removed her earphones. Ishir said, "Tanner is on this plane."

Ananya panicked instantly and asked, "What do we do now?"

Ishir explained the plan, "We don't have any luggage so as soon as we land, we will run away and walk inside the arrivals section. I have called for a car for ourselves. So, as soon as we get the car, we will drive all the way to Sarnath."

Ananya and Ishir were hoping for Tanner to not find and kill them inside the airplane or do anything to ruin their plan of finding the Ashokan symbols before he does. As soon as they land, the hunt for the second symbol shall begin.

# CHAPTER 25

**1:00 p.m.**
**Varanasi Airport**

With a rough, bumpy landing, the flight finally arrived their destination. Ishir, Ananya, and Dr. Tripathi were impatiently waiting for the boarding ramp to touch the door gates for them to run away from Tanner's sight. Ishir, Ananya, and Dr, Tripathi stood up from their seats, ready to leave and run. Tanner glanced at the three of them and called out Dr. Tripathi's name, "Ashwin! What a coincidence?" If humour was expressed by Tanner, the reaction in his mind was of worry and anxiety.

The three of them were right next to the door of the back of the plane. As soon as the air hostess allowed them to step out to the boarding ramp, the three of them ran like mice chased by a cat. Tanner tried pushing the crowded queue of the airplane but failed to do so. He had no choice but to wait in line till he and Cheng finally walked out on the boarding ramp. He noticed them running towards the bus. While Ishir was running with Ananya and Dr. Tripathi, he came up with a strategy which he instantly told them, "We will step inside the bus with one door and head outside the very next second through the back door." Dr. Tripathi and Ananya nodded in response. Ananya thought it may not be a great idea but she turned around and saw Tanner and another Asian man running with him. Ananya said to herself, 'Seems like there are two cats to chase three mice.' The bus doors were open. Ishir, Ananya, and Dr. Tripathi jumped inside. It was a challenge for Dr. Tripathi to run as he was a middle-aged man in his fifties carrying a paunch. Beads of sweat made him wipe his forehead with his handkerchief, he also decided to clean his glasses when Tanner jumped inside the bus with Cheng.

Ishir saw the bus filled. He grabbed Ananya and Dr. Tripathi by their hands and tossed them outside the bus along with himself. At the very moment Tanner was attempting to jump, the bus doors closed automatically and Tanner bumped into the door not being able to jump outside.

Ananya was furious at Ishir and yelled at him, "You idiot! Why did you throw me out?"

"That was part of the plan. It was great timing otherwise he would've caught us. So calm down, and let's head to the car," answered Ishir. The three of them stood inside another bus which took them to the arrivals section. The three of them anxiously walked outside the airport gates and found their car. The person who handed over the car was sent by Ishir's logistician with the Sword of Power named Eric Silva. He also gave him a brown-leathered duffel bag. He said, "Eric told me you might need this." Ishir took the bag and the three of them inside the blue sedan and drove off to Sarnath, which is on the outskirts of Varanasi. As soon as the car leaves the parking lot, Ishir looked at Tanner sitting inside a car. Ishir said, "Seems like Tanner has brought along a friend of his on this treasure hunt."

As soon as the two cars faced adjacent to each other, Ishir and Mark stared at each other giving a ferocious frown. Ishir firmly pressed his car's accelerator and started driving. Tanner followed Ishir's car. Soon, both the cars were rushing on the highway with greenery and farms on the banks of the road. Ananya turned around and asked, "Is that Tanner in the car?"

"Yes," replied Ishir with his focus on the road and his foot stuck to the accelerator. "You two are racing towards Sarnath?" asked Ananya wittily. Ishir replied, "It is more of him chasing me." Ananya looked at the brown-leathered duffel bag on the front seat besides Ishir. She leaned forward and pulled the bag to the back. She unzipped the bag looking for a gun and found herself a black 9 mm Beretta. She checked if the magazines were full and the safety lock was on. She turned the safety lock on and rolled the car window down.

The breezy wind blowing in her face tried to make her thick hair fly. Her head and her arms leaned outside the window. She was trying to focus and aim at Tanner's head so that this whole thing ends once and for all. She aimed and pressed the trigger only for the bullet to hit the right tire which was now punctured. The gentle teddy bear-like Ashwin had to pull her inside the car and shut the window to prevent the breezy wind from flowing inside. The shocked Ishir was still processing through what happened in the last thirty seconds. He was shocked but also impressed the way Ananya could stop Tanner from chasing them. Ishir asked, "Where did you learn that from?" "Bollywood," replied Ananya with a smirk.

About half an hour later, the three of them arrived at Sarnath. Sarnath was a Buddhist society located 10 kilometres away from Varanasi near the confluence of the Ganges and Varuna rivers in Eastern Uttar Pradesh. This is the Buddhist society where Gautam Buddha taught his first sermon of *'Dhammachakkapavatansutta'*—the Noble Eightfold path after attaining enlightenment at Bodh Gaya. In 12th century, when Turkish invaders made their way inside North India, they decided to destroy all Buddhist sites across North India. In year 1815, under British India, Colonel Colin Mackenzie, Major General Alexander Cunningham (the father of Indian archaeology), and Major Jonathan Duncan were one of the first few people to find out about it. The more they excavated, explored, and learnt about Sarnath, it led them to declaring it as an archaeological site under the Archaeological Survey of India (ASI).

Ananya looked at the various monuments at Sarnath searching for the exact location of the second Ashokan symbol. They must get hold of that symbol before Tanner interrupts once again. She took a glance at the large Buddhist site wondered where would they find the second symbol. She opened a folder from her bag and opened a few sheets of paper with 'Sarnath' titled on top with a small, rectangular post-it note for her research sheets and articles that were going to be submitted for her research paper on Ashoka. She wondered if the fragments of the Ashokan pillar had it. However, those fragments of pillars were caged and no one could cross that. She ran towards the monastery ruins in search of the symbol. In 1017, when Mahmud Ghazni's troops set foot inside Banaras, the monastery was also destroyed. She visualised that in the past, before the Ghaznavid army ruined the monastery, monks must have meditated in this very monastery possibly chanting the Buddhist mantra "Om Mani Padme Hum" or practicing the three refuges of Buddhism: the Buddha, the *Dharma,* the Sangha. She wondered if Hiuen Tsang studied here and also imagined The Ghaznavid troops galloping their troops inside Sarnath and attacking the people residing in Sarnath and the monuments such as the pillars. Visualising events from the past was Ananya's biggest strength and that is one of the reasons she enjoyed history. She looked around and found no such symbol, except a few inscriptions that she wanted to decipher, but Tanner was the only constraint and the inscriptions would have been deciphered and translated much before she was planning to.

"Our very own Indiana Jones should know that we are running out of time," joked Ishir as he looked at Ashwin.

"Call her here," said Ashwin.

Ishir shouted her name and told her to run towards them. The three of them were standing on the lawns with multiple ruined monuments and pillars surrounding them. Ashwin said, "If you fancy yourself to be Indiana Jones then I'm sure you can find the second symbol."

"I fancy myself as Robert Langdon but continue," joked Ananya as she referenced the famous character from the Dan Brown novels. Ashwin hinted, "Ashoka's second symbol is at the stupa that he built."

Ananya looked all around herself and found the Dhamek Stupa to be the closest, she pulled out the map of Sarnath from her bundle of documents and said, "It is the Dhamek Stupa. Let's go!" She sprinted from the Bodhi tree while Dr. Ashwin Tripathi was resting below the it. Ananya reached the Dhamek Stupa with Ishir right behind her.

The Dhamek Stupa built by Ashoka is one of the most visible structures in Sarnath. Excavations revealed that more than a dozen railing pillars were installed between the 2nd to 1st century BCE by the Shunga rulers, who were descendants of the Mauryan general Pushyamitra Shunga who assassinated the last ruler of the Mauryan dynasty Brihadhratha. Ananya said, "This is the stupa where Buddha gave his first sermon."

Ishir was confused, he asked, "Didn't Ashoka build this stupa? Decades after Buddha attained Nirvana?"

"Yes but this is the exact location where Buddha gave his first sermon of the Noble Eightfold path. When Ashoka converted to Buddhism, he built the Dhamek Stupa at the location where Buddha gave his first sermon commemorating his teachings of the 3 refuges and the Eightfold path." Ananya moved a few steps closer to the stupa and said, "Even though Ashoka built this stupa, there have been several dynasties who have made some modifications to it." She pointed towards a specific inscription. "This one is about the 40th year of the Kaushambi ruler Ashvagosha which was probably between 80 to 150 AD. The floral carvings date back to the Gupta empire's origin."

"What about the symbol?" asked Ishir.

"For such a huge stupa, finding a small symbol should be noticeable but also a little tough at the same time," replied Ananya.

Ananya carefully observed the entire stupa. She walked around the entire stupa and observed every detail until she noticed something unusual. A round golden symbol with the four lion Ashokan symbol was on the bottom most level of the stupa.

The symbol was right below the Dhamek Stupa. Ananya tried scratching the symbol, tapping it, but that did not seem to work. She kept the files back in her bag, and as she zipped the bag, she noticed a similar symbol on the book of Sociology that was given to Ananya by her professor.

She thought for a minute and removed the replicated golden symbol from that book. She tried to find the difference between the two symbols, she held the symbol closer to the golden symbol that lay right below the Dhamek stupa built by Ashoka. The symbol from the ground was pulled towards the symbol that Ananya was holding.

Ishir asked, "Is that some kind of a magnet?

Ananya said, "We never know I guess, we just need to get out of here before Tanner finds us."

* * *

Tanner and Cheng walked inside Sarnath. Tanner used the second map from the box of maps. He opened the map of Sarnath to find the second Ashokan symbol. As he observed the map, he told Cheng, "This map will help us find the second symbol.'"

"Does that mean you have the first one?" asked Cheng.

"Yes," Tanner unzipped his light brown leather satchel and slowly removed the first symbol which was shining and radiant. "Here. Two more of these and the manuscripts will be ours," said Tanner as he took another glance at the map. Cheng also took a look at the entire Sarnath map in Tanner's hand. He said, "There are three stupas here."

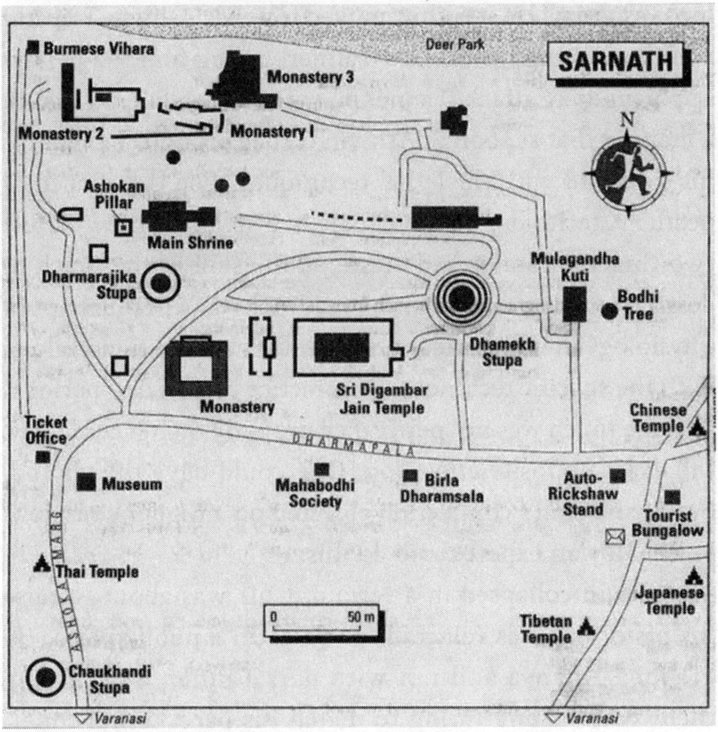


"There is the Dhamek stupa, besides that is the Dharmarajika stupa, and the Chaukhandi stupa."

"Ashoka built two of them. Let's check the Dhamek stupa," said Tanner. The two of them made their way from the Bodhi tree to the Dhamek stupa, as they were about to make the turn towards the Dhamek stupa, Tanner noticed Dr. Tripathi on the phone. He turned his head to the other side and saw Ananya and some other guy who tried attacking him yesterday. He stealthily moved towards Ashwin Tripathi who was facing his back to Tanner, giving him the perfect opportunity to attack. Tanner pointed his two fingers in such a manner that as soon as Ashwin turned around, Tanner hit his forehead with the lethal technique called the 'Touch of death'. A technique to kill people in a split second with just two fingers. Tanner had mastered the skill of the touch of death over the years when he read Ashwin's Manuscript of Physiology in which the touch of death was mentioned along with the specific technique and practice required to perform it. If the touch was not performed properly then it could give the exact opposite effect too. One could have their mind, brain, and soul's connection elevated on a higher conscious level. Only an expert could do this.

Ashwin collapsed in a second. Ishir was about to raise his pistol but was reluctant to do so in a public place. He grabbed Ananya and ran with her. Tanner was chasing them with Cheng trying to match his pace with Tanner. While the people around who ran towards Ashwin's dead body were waiting for an ambulance, Ishir and Ananya were being chased by Tanner and some Asian guy they had not see before. Ishir opened the door for Ananya in a hurry and jumped on the car's bonnet to slide down to the other end of the car. He opened the door of the driver's seat and started the car to reach the hotel as soon as possible. Tanner tried stopping him in the way but Ishir was not going to hesitate running him down. So, Tanner did the usual thing that happens in action movies, which was climbing on the bonnet, the sunroof, and then jumping on the concrete road once again. Ishir drove his car from Sarnath to the hotel. Tanner could not follow him because they had arrived by cab. The second Ashokan symbol has been found, the last one lay in Bihar.

# CHAPTER 26

**Rinpoche's Chambers**

"Dr. Ashwin Tripathi has been murdered. Only four members of the Nine Unknown remain," said Dr. Schmidt with a poker face showing absolutely no reaction and no emotions as he received a text message from Ananya. Apart from Schmidt who was hiding his fear within him, everyone else in the room was shocked. The Preserver of the Nine had an iota of fear at the back of his brain in spite of saying that destiny is the best writer. He decided to follow that by surrendering himself to the higher powers and destiny itself.

About a minute of grieving later, Dr. Paula Maxwell received a phone call from Ishir. She swiped to answer the ring. "Hi Ishir, you are on speakerphone with the four of us."

Ishir began without exchanging pleasantries as he knew there isn't time for it. "You must have received my message by now about Dr. Ashwin; I called for an ambulance after we left immediately. Turns out Mark Tanner and Cheng were at Sarnath too, not only that, we had a bit of an exchange of pleasantries at the Varanasi airport too." Ishir continued, "I think that your phones might be tapped so let me tell you this. I am coming over there. Tanner coming to that location and attempting to steal the symbol is inevitable. So, let's stop him over there."

"Trust me. I have a plan," said Ananya over the phone.

Ishir disconnected the call and asked Ananya, "What exactly is your plan?"

"We give Tanner the symbol," replied Ananya briefly.

"Are you crazy? Give him the symbol? Are you out of your mind?" shouted Ishir.

"Do you trust me?" asked Ananya with a puppy face.

Ishir smiled, scratched his hair, took a moment to think, and lied "'No. Absolutely not."

* * *

Back at the secret conference room at Rinpoche's residence. Guru Rinpoche said, "We never had this thing called the Saviour of the Nine. Only Guru Rinpalga was the true saviour of these manuscripts. I told Nivedita Kaur that this would be a bad idea but she wanted to ensure that the Nine Unknown are fully safe, and who better than a former MI6 spy? But look how the tables have turned. I could use my key but Tanner coming here seems inevitable after all. Who was this man on the phone?" asked the Preserver.

Dr. Gokhale introduced Ishir to the Rinpoche. "Ishir Singh, a former RAW agent who has this organisation that he runs to carry out unsanctioned and unauthorised missions on RAW's payroll as an independent logistics handler. Considering that we are a secret society and this remains between us, then this too shall be a secret. Apparently, only the RAW chief has knowledge of the existence of the Nine Unknown which is why Ishir's assignment is to save us from this looming danger."

* * *

Ananya took a silent dramatic gasp and said, "Well you have to. There is no choice."

Ishir smiled and said, "Fine I do trust you."

Ishir removed his burner phone from his pocket and removed a small USB-like looking device from his bag and inserted it to the charging port of his phone. He dialled Tanner's number from Ananya's phone, awaiting for the ring to be answered.

* * *

Mark Tanner had reached his hotel, as he walked inside the lobby of the hotel with Cheng Zhang, just about to set his foot inside the elevator, he received a phone call from an unknown number which could not be detected by any caller-detecting software. Tanner answered the phone call. "Who's this?"

"If you want the second symbol, then meet me on the banks of the Raja Harishchandra Ghat," said Ishir as he placed a voice-altering pen towards his neck. Tanner asked, "What time?"

"5:30 p.m.,'" said the boat-horn-sounding voice.

Tanner hung up and looked at his watch. He had two hours to reach the location. The same number dialled on his phone once again. Tanner answered it for the second time. The voice began, "I hope you know that there are no free lunches. I too want something in return, you fool! Get me the previous nine manuscripts in exchange for the symbol," said Ishir.

"Why should I trust you?" asked the British-accented renegade spy.

"Is there anyone else you know who has the second symbol? Besides me?" asked Ishir rhetorically and hung up the phone call.

"You sound more villainy than Tanner himself," laughed Ananya.

Ishir carefully took the symbol from Ananya who took it out from her bag. Ishir placed the symbol inside his pocket, as soon as he was about to leave, Ananya volunteered herself to accompany Ishir for this dangerous mission, in spite of him denying her. Ananya persisted, leaving Ishir no choice but to allow her to be a part of this mission. Ananya argued about not being allowed to be a part of the mission just because she is a woman and Ishir a man. Ishir clarified that he did not want Ananya to lose her life, and that she is a civilian who does not have any formal training to operate with firearms. Not just that, Ananya had a plan for which she had to stay alive.

* * *

**5:30 p.m.**
**Harishchandra Ghat**
**Varanasi**

Ishir was standing on the steps of the huge stone staircases of the Harishchandra Ghat in Varanasi. He was waiting for Mark Tanner with the nine manuscripts which he is supposed to exchange with the second Ashokan symbol. In front of Ishir, there were pyres of dead bodies burning. People were often cremated at the Harishchandra Ghat so that the soul of the dead bodies could attain salvation. After the bodies are burnt, the ashes are poured in the Holy river of the Ganges or Ganga as it is believed that the soul will be transported to heaven and will escape the cycle of rebirth. King Harishchandra of Ayodhya was the epitome of someone who always followed truth. Which is why bodies are burnt at the Harishchandra and the Manikarnika Ghat as it is one of the steps of attaining eternal liberation or *moksha.* As Ishir looked at the bodies burning, he realised that death is after all inevitable and should be celebrated as much as life is. That death is a part of life, a truth that should be accepted.

He remembered a line from the Bhagavad Gita which he read after his divorce, "Those who are born must die one day."

As he looked at the holy river of Ganga, he saw Mark Tanner on a boat. As soon as the boat reached the banks of the Harishchandra ghat, he climbed up the stairs, avoiding all the funeral pyres and the fires flaming on the pyres. Ishir looked at Mark Tanner and nodded, Tanner nodded back. Tanner handed over a brown-leathered satchel and said, "These are the manuscripts." Ishir took out a symbol looking like a gold coin and showed it to Tanner. "This is Ashoka's symbol."

"I understand that you want to ruin my plan and safeguard Ashoka's Secret. But I will find it by hook or by crook."

Tanner bended over to reach his ankle and pulled out his small black revolver. Ishir kicked Tanner in his knees. The bag rolled over the staircase. Ishir jumped to grab his hands on the satchel containing the manuscripts and tossed the symbol in the air which sinks inside the water near the bank of the river. Ishir put the sling of the satchel on his shoulder and scurried away from the ghat, taking big leaps on the huge steps of the ghat's staircase. With some difficulty climbing up, he finally made it to the top of the staircase and ran towards the narrow alleyways of Varanasi.

Tanner jumped inside the river, he put his hand inside the water of the river, struggling to find the symbol, he reached his fingers to touch the river bed. Mark finally found the symbol. His trousers and shoes got wet with the water drenching his shoes insoles and his black trousers till the knee-length too got drenched and heavy for Mark to run. Mark was struggling to climb up the huge stone-structured stairs of the ghat while grabbing the symbol and carefully placing it inside his yellow-lemon shirt's breast pocket. He made his way outside the ghat to chase Ishir who was about a hundred meters away from him running. Ishir wanted to run towards the parking lot, Tanner was following him. Both of them had flashbacks of their car chase on the highway from the Varanasi airport, however this time it was a run chase.

Tanner was trying not to limp as he chased Ishir. Ishir was about to lose his breath but continued running. The adrenaline rush of flight was catching onto the both of them. As Tanner was chasing Ishir on the busy narrow street, he called up Cheng and told him to start the car. Ishir pressed his wireless Bluetooth earpiece to activate his voice assistant Siri on his iPhone. He told Siri to call up Ananya. As soon as Ananya answered the ring, the sprinting Ishir said, "I'm being chased by Tanner, start the car!"

Ananya asked, "Why don't you just kill him?"

"This is not the time to argue! I am in the middle of a dramatic run chase and I am running out of breath so just start the car! If I kill Tanner then the guys paying him will get another Tanner or just a hundred other Tanners! Start the car!" explained Ishir panting. The two of them dodged many the vendors and jumped over various carts and bulldozered over all the people crowding up the entire street. As they were about to reach the parking lot, Cheng saw Ananya and quickly ran towards her vehicle. He smashed the glass of the driver seat's car with his bare fist and pulled her hair to pull her outside the car. He pointed a gun to her head. As Ishir reached the parking lot, he saw Ananya being held hostage on gunpoint by this unknown Asian man. Ananya knocked Cheng's nose by smacking it with her head. Cheng pulled the trigger, but the bullet went past Ananya's hair. She went blank for a second as she saw a ray of light glowing in front of her eyes from a tunnel. About seven seconds later when she realised that Cheng's nose was bleeding, she elbowed his neck resulting him in collapsing on the floor and choking.

Ishir took her inside the car, to the front seat and slid on the bonnet to the driving seat. Ananya got out of the car and said, "I am driving." She sat inside the car and fastened the seat belt. The engine had already started. Suddenly, Tanner stood in front of their car, who had reached and was catching for breath. Ananya had already started the car. Tanner jumped on the bonnet, then the roof and fell on the floor to save his life from getting blown by a car. He limped towards Cheng and saw that he was dead. As Ananya and Ishir's car was about to make its way towards the hotel, she asked, "When is our next flight to Patna?"

"Tomorrow morning. Also it is a train journey so that Tanner won't get suspicious and the last thing he will do is travel by the Indian Railways because he has to race against time," said Ishir.

# CHAPTER 27

**1136 AD**
**Nalanda University**

Nalanda University was one of the earliest universities to be established in ancient India. The university's structure was held in a *gurukul* format where students would select a specific subject(s) to study and there will be a professor allotted to them for it. Most subjects were interdisciplinary studies taught as philosophies. The students would wake up early in the morning and head towards the wide and vast lawn where yoga practices would be held starting with morning meditations which would take place followed by some yoga exercises such as the *suryanamaskars* or sun-salutations. The sun was shining bright and the *shishyas* or students were switching between classes. Most classes were usually commenced in the outdoors. After that, there were a few classes and research work that would take place in the library. It was business as usual for Nalanda

University, until Bakhtiyar Khilji's hordes had reached the gates of Nalanda.

The neighing of Khilji's horse, followed by the sound of the stroking of his sharp sword killing a student, along with the sound of students screaming while running helter-skelter, alarmed Tenzing Rinpalga, a professor of Physiology at Nalanda University and the head of the Nine Unknown. He was writing his Manuscript of Physiology while conducting some research from the manuscripts inked on dried palm leaves inside the bookshelves of Nalanda's gigantic library. Rinpalga rushed towards the restriction section of Nalanda's prestigious library and carefully removed a chest. The chest was none other than Ashoka's Secret. Rinpalga's colleagues—three members of the Nine Unknown rushed inside the library and informed Rinpalga, "Five members are dead. It is just us. The Remaining Four."

Rinpalga and his other four managed to sneak outside the huge campus of the Nalanda University with their heads covered in the Buddhist cotton robes. As soon as they reached on top of a hill near Nalanda's campus. They could see the university's library burning. The library contained sacred texts of infinite knowledge. They still had the job of preserving the chest. The Remaining Four travelled all the way from Nalanda University in Magadh to the caves in Tibet in a fortnight. From travelling in a humid climate in Magadh to getting lost on the way in the midst of the deserts of Gandhar to crossing Mount Kailash's beautiful Mansarovar lake and finally making their way to one of the Buddhist caves near Kailash with the breezy cold weather surrounded with snow and showering snowfalls.

The Remaining Four members had travelled with their head covered in the saffron yellow and red Buddhist robes across all biomes and climatic temperatures. Rinpalga addressed the three other members of the Nine Unknown, "The Nine Unknown Men..." Taking a pause, he resumed, "has been reduced to us Remaining Four. When we travelled all the way from Gandhar, we noticed how the Turks have made their way inside our land. The knowledge inside this manuscripts has been saved by us. The knowledge inside these Nine manuscripts is possibly a thousand years ahead of this time. Our job is to preserve, protect, research, and update all these manuscripts for the betterment of humanity. They better not get into the wrong hands." The three monks nodded in agreement. Rinpalga continued, "The alchemist Brahmadhvaja should create three golden symbols which will have the four lion Ashokan symbol. This golden symbol resembling a golden coin will be installed in three places. The first symbol shall be placed in the Topra Pillar in the Pong Ghati near the Yamunanagar district. The second symbol shall be placed at the Dhamek Stupa in Kashi, and the third and final symbol shall be placed inside the Lomas Rishi Cave. The alchemist Brahmadhvaja must also design three keys. One key shall be passed from one head of the Nine Unknown to the new head of the Nine Unknown. The other key is to be found at the same location that the last symbol is meant to be found."

One of the four scholars belonging to the Nine Unknown asked, "What about the third key?"

"We need to start recruiting five other members. I must cartograph a map. Rather, three maps, to be passed down from the previous head to the new head of the Nine Unknown in order to locate the second key. And there shall be one map in one of the monasteries in Tibet to locate the Ashoka's Secret over here if someone is in dire need of these manuscripts for a positive purpose."

# CHAPTER 28

**1976**
**Lhasa**
**Tibet**

Yao Zhi was visiting Tibet decades after Tibet had been annexed by the Chinese forces after the Chinese Communist Party came into power. It was the period of cold war when the Soviet Union had expanded its ideology of communism and the United States of America was expanding the ideology of capitalism, only to prove their superiority. Countries like China, Vietnam, and Laos were already following USSR's footsteps.

Yao was visiting Tibet as a part of an assignment to teach as a visiting professor in Tibet. After his month-long stay, he was planning to go back to his home in Guangzhou. He decided to study and conduct some research in the university's library while he is there. The library contained several books about Buddhism and Buddhist studies. None of the bookshelves had books which interested him. So, he decided to stealthily sneak his way inside the dusty shelves of the restricted section.

He came across a book that interested him titled, 'Ashoka's Nine'. He picked it up from the bookshelf and carefully sneaked out of the restricted section to one of the long wooden tables in the library. Considering that it was an old book with dust and dated pieces of paper. He asked for a pair of gloves and tweezers to carefully open the 300–400 year old book. The librarian handed him a pair of white latex gloves and tweezers. Yao wore the white latex gloves with a hint of a powder texture inside them and took the tweezers with him to open the book. As soon as he opened the very first page of the book, dust flew up, reaching inside his nose and causing him to sneeze.

The university's library always kept a pair of gloves and tweezers handy to study their old, dusty dated typewritten books and handwritten manuscripts. Yao had to bear the dust of the book he was reading, which he found quite interesting. As Yao turned each page after a few seconds of reading them, he got to know more about Ashoka's Nine. A secret society founded by an Indian emperor named Ashoka, the Buddhist king of India who converted to Buddhism after seeing the horrors of the Kalinga war.

The more he read about Ashoka's Nine, the more he was intrigued about Ashoka and his secret society. He read that the Nine Unknown will study nine subjects and their job is to research, update, and protect these nine manuscripts for the betterment of humanity. The knowledge inside these nine manuscripts was so powerful.

Yao flipped on to another page to know more about the Nine Unknown. Turns out there was another chapter to dig deeper about the Nine Unknown in a bold font and underline titled, “Ashoka’s Secret”. He read that the manuscripts are hidden inside a large wooden chest called ‘Ashoka’s Secret’. The wooden chest can be opened with a key. There are differently designed keys that can open this chest with each key carved of the four-lioned Ashokan symbol as the handle of the key, and ‘𑀅𑀰𑁄𑀓’ is engraved on the key which translated to “Ashoka” in the Roman Harvard–Kyoto method of translating the Brahmi script to English. The next paragraph mentioned that Ashoka’s Secret is inside a hidden cave behind a monastery which is at the distance of one kilometre from the monastery.

Yao instantly made up his mind to embark on the treasure hunt to find Ashoka’s Secret. He tore the piece of paper from the book, “Ashoka’s Nine”, carefully folded it and hid it inside his blazer’s silky flapped jetted pocket and walked outside the library towards his residential quarters for the visiting staff. He made up his mind to find the Ashoka’s Secret and actually verify if it is a myth, a fictional story, or a secret safeguarded inside a Tibetan cave. He decided to embark on this quest once the weekend starts.

As soon as he reached the residential quarters, he removed his blazer and hung it on one of the chairs of the small dining tables made with glass. Apart from his living room and bathroom, his studio apartment which was given to him as his residence was in a complete mess consisting of clothes, empty food packets, books, and large bundles of scribbled notes on white printing paper. There were uncountable sheets of paper. Yao cracked a joke that the amount of sheets of paper inside his house resembled to the entire population of China.

Yao waited patiently for the weekend to arrive so that he can embark on the journey of that mysterious hidden cave that preserves all secrets. He opened his wardrobe made of oak wood. He crouched towards the bottom of the wardrobe to his safe, and slowly and carefully pressed each button to show a numerical code with all nine digits in Chinese. Yao opened the safe and opened a black and grey-coloured revolver. He opened the barrel of the revolver to check if all seven bullets are inside the barrel. Yao always kept his revolver for safety and this was the first time he was using it. He hid his revolver in his trousers' pocket and walked out of his residence with the key in his jacket's zip pocket and a bag containing some snacks, a bottle of water, and two boxes of juice.

As soon as Yao was about to close his door, he realised he had forgotten something. He rushed towards his dining table where his cobalt blue blazer was hanging on the chair. He removed the blazer from the chair and took out the folded piece of paper from the jetted pocket inside his black jacket's zip pocket. He threw the blazer on the dining table and walked out of his apartment building. His search for the chest had just begun.

At first, Yao decided to walk to a bus station. He booked his ticket for one of the nearby towns closer to the monastery on the snowy mountains of Lhasa, which would lead to the secret cave as per the torn page. After several hours of travelling by bus, he finally reached a village called Siddharth Nagar. No bus could travel beyond Siddharth Nagar. The farthest a vehicle could travel to reach the monastery was the very village that Yao had reached. The last point for any vehicle. One only had the choice to climb mountains because there were no roads to reach that monastery.

Yao asked one of the local street food sellers who was busy preparing a local Tibetan dish called *thukpa* which was a type of a hot Tibetan soup mixed with spices and buckwheat noodles. A food that suited perfectly for the weather. Yao was hungry and his stomach was rumbling. He ordered the *thukpa* and after enjoying the deliciously hot soup, he asked the *thukpa* seller about the mountain monastery. He said that it would take about twelve hours or more to reach there. Yao looked at his gold and silver analogue watch to check the time. It was 12:00 PM, he had already finished his lunch which gave him enough warmth and energy to climb the mountain. Yao made his way inside the village to buy some more food, especially three packets of the Tibetan dumplings called *momos.* He walked inside the market to buy a small mattress and a blanket and off he went to his trek.

About a day later, Yao finally reached the mountain monastery. The hills were steep and difficult to climb. He wondered how could anyone in in their right mind think of creating an entire monastery on the snowy mountains. The snowfall was heavier compared to the village and the breeze was blowing strongly. Yao finally made his way inside the monastery, he looked very weak and tired. Looking at his exhausted condition, the monks decided to arrange a warm meal for him. After Yao ate his meal, he asked one of the abbots (head) of the monastery, "Where is the Ashoka cave?"

The abbot of the Buddhist monastery looked at two of his loyal disciples. In his baritone, old man-voice, he said, "I am afraid I haven't heard of such cave."

"I saw how you stared at your men for a few seconds indicating that you may be surprised as to how I know about such a cave. A hidden cave."

"Are you a part of the Nine Unknown?" asked the abbot.

Yao took a moment to pause and pretended like he was a part of the Nine Unknown. "Yes. You may not have heard of me but I am a part of them. I joined recently."

"Fine. There is an underground route right behind the meditation room which can be opened with a key. If you are not claustrophobic then you can walk across that underground tunnel for about a few kilometres till you find yourself a ladder. You climb the ladder, and there will be a circular latch which you have to rotate anti-clockwise three times and you will be able to open this underground door. Just a few feet ahead of that is the cave. We will also give you a symbol through which you can open the cave and you will find yourself the chest."

Yao walked through the corridors of the monastery to reach the meditation room. The meditation room was more of an enclosed amphitheatre with the seat in the middle belonging to the abbot and a large white-marble statue of the meditating Buddha at the back of the abbot's cushioned meditating seat. Yao, the monastery's abbot, and his disciple walked towards the Buddha's statue and carefully made their way towards the white-coloured door which matched the wall's paint. The abbot unlocked the white-coloured door and opened it. The disciple reached out to give him a round and golden symbol looking like a gold coin with the engraving of the common four-lioned Ashokan symbol. Before Yao took it, the abbot stopped him and asked, "What is the chest called?"

"Ashoka's Secret," replied Yao. The abbot allowed the disciple to give the key to Yao. Yao carefully put the symbol inside his pocket and walked towards the ladder. There was no light, he just had to keep walking till he felt the ladder blocking him. Yao walked but thought that walking was not making this treasure hunt interesting. So, he decided to sprint as much as he could.

On the other hand, while Yao was sprinting till he felt a roped ladder on a stone wall, the abbot told his disciple inside the meditation room as they closed the door, "Follow him, be careful and hide from him. My intuition tells me that this man does not have the key and nor is he a part of the Nine."

"Why do you think he is not a part of the Nine ?" asked the disciple.

The abbot answered, "That cave has been closed for the three hundred years. After that, an entirely new and fresh place for the manuscripts was introduced and the hidden Ashoka cave were almost forgotten about."

"But how do you know that?" asked the disciple.

"Every abbot of this mountain monastery knows about this cave and the chest. The last time there was any contact established was three decades ago, when I was just a newly-joined monk. Go there, reach before he does and hide, it is highly unlikely that he is a member of the Nine. So once you get there, ensure the manuscripts cease to exist and so does that man."

The disciple ran from the gates of the monastery and ran in the snowy, breezy weather of the mountains till he made his way to the Ashoka cave. The disciple and the other abbots were shocked at how the abbot resorted to violence in such a situation. But then the both of them understood why he chose this. When it came to preserving and safeguarding a secret which is doing great wonders for the betterment of humanity, it was necessary to resort to violence for someone who intended to use it for the wrong purpose.

About a few minutes later, Yao finally found his way to the ladder. He climbed up the ladder and noticed a round latch which he spun in an anti-clockwise direction by sticking his legs and one hand to the ladder. He opened the underground door which flapped open the snow. He made his way out of the door inviting himself to a mighty breeze blowing heavy wind in his face. He walked towards the cave which had been blocked by a gigantic rock. Yao removed the symbol from his pocket and placed it on the carved circular area where it was meant to be placed. The rock moved towards the right on its own. Yao was amazed by the mechanism of that kind for a special door made for securing the chest inside. He saw a painting of two Buddhist deities called—the Chakrasamvara, a male deity which was painted in blue, and a deity painted in red was a female deity called Vajrayogini, below which was the chest. By the time Yao made it inside the cave, the abbot's disciple saw the cave's rock moving aside. He assumed that Yao was inside and he had to hide for the element of surprise. Yao saw a wooden chest which consisted of a keyhole inside it. He knew he could not open it so he decided to put a good use of his revolver. He aimed the revolver at it and fired four rounds on the chest. The chest did not open. The disciple chanted something in his mind and summoned a mantra to invoke fire in his hand which he aimed at the chest, for it to blow up in fire and smoke in seconds.

Yao who unknowingly dodged the fire attack was in the state of shock for a second. He fired the last three rounds of his revolver which killed the disciple. Yao was furious at how the manuscripts blew up in the air. However, there were a few pages which he collected. He looked at the dead body of the disciple and said, "The truth always reveals itself. No matter how much you suppress it."

Yao read the page about how the body can elevate itself to a divine state that it can summon celestial weapons to invoke fire, light, water, and air. He read another page about the designs of Pushpak Vimana, and finally he read a page about the touch of death. About a few months later, Yao handed these pages to the MSS director Lee Zhang, the father of Cheng Zhang. Little did Yao know that the Sword of Power were just one step closer to getting their hands at Ashoka's Secret with the help of the key.

# CHAPTER 29

**Patna**
**Bihar**

Tanner managed to safely land to Patna; however, he was unsure of how will he be able to get out of it with the key and his life safely. Soon, Tanner walked out of the airport and received his car which was one of the old jeeps. He started driving with the air conditioner not working. After a bit of driving, he came to realise that it was not just the air conditioner alone, it was also his breaks, and the steering wheel as well as the tires which were lame enough to work. Tanner had reached in the midst of Patna as he kept driving, he came across a herd of cattle which gave him no choice but to turn the steering to the right which led to the jeep crashing on the walls of a narrow lane.

Tanner picked up his satchel and jumped out of the jeep. The jeep had already caught some smoke. Tanner apologised to the local crows and just walked away. He looked around the streets of Patna and noticed a certain change in atmosphere, the city looked like a pool of visual pollution. He heard a lot of vehicles creating noise and flashing lights. He looked at the corner of the city and noticed an auto rickshaw stand with multiple auto rickshaws lined up in a chain. These were not the usual two-three seaters, these were six passenger seaters. Tanner looked across and saw a bunch of streetside stalls serving the local dish *litti chokha* made of mashed eggplant and stuffed potato.

Tanner was a few blocks away from where he had crashed his malfunctioned, rather barely functioning, jeep. A group of men were observing him from one of the local eateries. They were discussing amongst themselves to rob him because he seemed like he would have money. Primarily because he seemed like a foreign tourist with a satchel and a fanny pack tied around his waist. These men chewing tobacco started running behind Tanner with guns. Tanner removed his pistol and fired a few bullets at them before he ran to safety. He kept running till there was no sight of another man chasing him with a gun.

Tanner stopped to take a breath. He bent down with his hands on his waist to take a few deep breaths. He was panting like a dog. After being able to breathe normally, he opened a map and to his surprise, he was standing right in front of the final location to find Ashoka's key. There was a black stone board with the words written in gold which said "Lomas Rishi Caves", also known as the "Barabar Caves". These caves were one of the most significant caves of the Bodh

Gaya. These caves were man-made and were built during Ashoka's reign for Buddhist pilgrims. This cave consisted two important objects: the third symbol and Ashoka's key.

Tanner walked inside the cave and it was just a room consisting of several Buddhist inscriptions. He walked on the entire property of the Barabar caves till he found the cave where the key was hiding. The Barabar caves consisted of smaller caves within itself such as the Sudama caves, Karan Chaupar caves, Vishwakarma caves, and the Lomas Rishi caves. During Ashoka's reign, there were nine Buddhist scholars who had access to this cave until 1136 AD, when Bakhtiyar Khilji's troops galloped inside Magadh and burnt the Nalanda library along with killing several Hindu, Buddhist, and East Asian scholars arriving from China, Burma, and Bhutan. The Nine Unknown men decided to go into hiding till they were discovered by a British officer named Stockton Mundy who discovered Ashoka's nine manuscripts containing such deep knowledge, much ahead of its time. And, an army officer named Major Duncan who translated certain Ashokan inscriptions near the Dhamek Stupa mentioning nine men who possessed potent knowledge with the purpose to help in the advancement of humanity.

Tanner was feeling sweaty as he walked inside the cave which was very long room with minimal exposure of natural light. As he reached the Lomas Rishi caves, he looked around that cave and found himself three circular carvings, each carving specifically in the shape of the fourth

Ashokan lion made on the back of the symbol. There was already one symbol placed which meant that all Tanner had to do was place the other two symbols in his fanny pack. Tanner unzipped his fanny pack and removed the two golden Ashokan symbols and carefully placed them on the circular gaps. Once he placed the symbols, a rectangular tile opened itself from which a golden key fell on the ground. Tanner reached towards the key and picked it up from the ground. He wiped it off with his white handkerchief. He looked at the key and saw the four lions of Ashoka as the handle of the key and a pointed edge which helped open Ashoka's Secret with a Brahmi inscription: '𑀅𑀰𑁄𑀓' which translated to "Ashoka" from the Roman Harvard–Kyoto method.

Tanner safely kept the key inside his fanny pack so that the key remains with him at all times, he walked out of the cave and thought out loud, "Burton, here I come."

# CHAPTER 30

**12:00 p.m.**
**Patna**

Ananya and Ishir arrived at Patna. As soon as their flight landed, Ananya called Dr. Gokhale. She picked up the phone and said, "Have you reached Gaya?"

"I'm about to," replied Ananya.

"'As soon as you reach Mahabodhi, wait near the Bodhi tree, there will be someone who will give something to you. He will give you two things. You will need them to reach here."

Ananya asked, "What are those things? Why will I need them? Can't you send me your location?"

"Now is not the time for questions Ananya!" said Dr. Gokhale and hung up the phone. The airport was getting crowded with people. A black sedan arrived for Ishir and Ananya, the both of them sat inside the car. They were not carrying any luggage because in the past two days, all they had done was run around and the only thing Ananya had been carrying was her pistachio green leather bag with her straps constantly on her shoulders as it contained potentially useful information for their mission.

Ishir drove the car while Ananya was going through some of her files that she used for her research. She opened up a few pieces of paper containing the information about Gaya and the Mahabodhi Temple built by Ashoka. She looked at the words and maps about the entire layout of Bodh Gaya and visualised Buddha attaining enlightenment under the Mahabodhi tree and sharing knowledge about peace, harmony, and enlightenment with the Sangha. She visualised Buddhists meditating upon the three refuges of Buddhism: "Buddham Sharanam Gacchami, Sangham Sharanam Gacchami, Dhammam Sharanam Gacchami."

Ananya stepped into that visual and looked outside the urbanised infrastructure of Gaya which was doing well for itself as a tier-two city. She time-lapsed and imagined if this was all a jungle in the past. They reached the city of Gaya, and as they moved closer and closer towards their location, they witnessed two tall statues of Buddha. One was a meditating-one painted in white and the other was a resting Buddha. Both statues were on different locations, but as their car was about to reach the Bodh Gaya area, they could notice these statues from a distance.

Ananya walked inside the property and her pace accelerated faster as she headed towards the Bodh Gaya tree. As she halted looking at the tree, she could see monks beneath it meditating upon the three refuges of Buddhism. Just as she had imagined, it was a similar visual to try time-lapsing into the time when Buddha was alive. Little did she know that the image she visualised would be actualised. The monks were meditating on the repetition of the familiar three refuges: "Buddham Sharanam Gacchami. Sangham Sharanam Gacchami, Dhammam Sharanam Gacchami."

A monk meditating noticed the presence of someone. He got up from his place and quietly moved outside the sea of the monks meditating. He handed over a rolled piece of paper and a bronze box to them. "I was told that you will arrive here. You will need these," said the monk as the other monks were busy meditating and chanting. They did not notice that a monk had gotten up from his place. Ishir opened the rolled up piece of paper and as he opened it, he saw a map. He asked the monk, "Why can't we use a GPS?"

The monk smiled as calmly as he always did. He replied, "Even in this digital world, you will never be able to find this monastery. It is located in a remote location that only a few people are aware about this monastery."

Ananya asked, "What's in the box?"

"Keep it with you for safety. Otherwise bury it," said the monk. He smiled at them and said "God bless!" which was cue for Ananya and Ishir to leave before any of the other monks found out about it. They used the map to direct towards the location of the monastery. After about ten minutes, the car embarked on a hill towards a monastery located in the midst of a hill surrounded by forests.

After the long car ride from Patna to Gaya, they finally made it to the location. The location was a Buddhist monastery located above a steep slope made of concrete which was meant to be climbed not possible to reach using a vehicle. Ananya climbed up the concrete slope and reached the monastery. She walked through the main entry doors of the monastery leading her to a giant meditation room consisting of dozens of monks donned in red and yellow Buddhist robes. There were about a hundred and seven monks and the monk in the middle was none other than the Preserver. All 108 monks were chanting "Om Mani Padme Hum" repeatedly, which created a sense of a vibration producing a certain energy; that is what Ananya felt as she listened to the mantra. The location was not Gaya, it was another monastery that was away from the Mahabodhi temple. This monastery on a hill in the midst of a remote forest which preserved Ashoka's Secret. In the middle of the monastery was giant meditation room which looked like an enclosed amphitheatre-like structure where all the hundred and seven monks were surrounding the one seat in the middle who was the Rinpoche. The structure mirrored ones like the mountain monastery in Tibet.

Shilpa Dixit took Ananya and Ishir from the giant room where the monks were meditating and brought them inside a library. The Remaining Four and the duo of Ananya and Ishir were inside the monastery where Ashoka's Secret lies. When the three of them entered the room, Leena introduced Ananya and Ishir to the present scenario, "This is where Ashoka's Secret is hidden."

"How and why is he linked to the Nine?" asked Ananya.

"One of the monasteries guarding an old set of manuscripts had been found. He was one of the monks who arrived to India from that monastery," said Leena as she whispered onto Ananya's ear.

"What do you mean by an old set?" asked Ananya.

"When Tibet had been annexed by China, the pathway to that monastery had been closed. We cut all ties from that monastery, and the Nine Unknown had to start all over again. This time, we decided to preserve the manuscripts in the very place that had been built by Ashoka," explained Leena as she continued whispering with Ananya.

"So what do we do till then?" asked Ishir as he eavesdropped the conversation between two women.

The Remaining Four and Ananya took some time to think. Ananya came up with a plan. "Whenever Tanner enters, let us know. We need to get the key from him."

Ananya took a moment to remember. "Professor Kaur gave me a key! I remember now!" She unzipped her bag and pulled out a black-coloured cuboid box. She carefully opened the black carboarded lid and there it was, Ashoka's first key which is always with the head of the Nine Unknown. Ananya looked at the key and said, "But Tanner still has the manuscripts, the old ones. We need to get those from him."

"But why?" asked Dr. Gokhale.

"I have a plan," said Ananya.

* * *

Tanner made his way to Gaya with a key in his fanny pack. After a long drive, about a hundred kilometres away from Patna was the very monastery where Ashoka's Secret had been hidden. Tanner made it easy for himself to track the location down as he had installed a tracking software on Ananya's device which is why he rented a jeep from someone in Patna and drove all the way towards Gaya. He felt that there was no use of the manuscripts and decided to burn them after he found the key in the Lomas Rishi caves. He safely managed to get himself out of there too. As he made his way out of Patna, he said to himself, "From Chandragupta's Pataliputra to the Bihar run by goons and dacoits. A bloody pitfall." The conditions in Bihar reminded him of a movie called "Mississippi Burning".

Now that Mark Tanner was at the final destination, he felt that his objective was about to be reached. He rode all the way from Patna to Bodh Gaya on a stolen motorcycle. He had to ride the motorcycle up the hill in order to reach the library, the final destination of Ashoka's Secret. There were dozens of monks near the Bodh Gaya and the Mahabodhi complex. As Tanner rode his bike further, the number of people decreased. By the transition of the decrease in fewer monks, he realised that he was getting closer to this unknown library which was a few kilometres away from Bodh Gaya. He had heard about this very library and how there are very few people who are aware of it, primarily the Nine Unknown, the Preserver, and the Preserver's few loyal disciples who took an oath to protect their Guru Rinpoche and this library for the betterment of humanity. The Rinpoche who arrived as a monk from Tibet, made his way towards Dharamshala first and after procuring Ashoka's Secret and the manuscripts inside it from a hidden library in Dharamshala, he believed that it would be better to store them in a hidden library at Gaya.

The unknown library in Gaya was initially an abandoned monastery located on a hill where no one visited. This is because the monks who were practicing Buddhist spirituality in that monastery had migrated to Dharamshala. When the Rinpoche got to know about this monastery from his fellow monks, he immediately established contact with the Nine Unknown through a secret telegram system and the moment the then-head of the Nine agreed upon relocating Ashoka's Secret, the Rinpoche moved the chest and travelled all the way to this unknown monastery near Gaya to set up a library and store Ashoka's Secret. The secret telegramming system was quite unknown and difficult to understand. The telegrams were written in a language which was a mix of the old and advanced Pali, Prakrit, and Brahmi code words, which was only familiar with the Nine Unknown and no one else. Not even historians, monks, or researchers who had knowledge about these scripts, were able to decipher the correspondence that was shared between the Nine Unknown.

On the small platform of that library, Ishir sipped on to his cup of tea made of earthen clay. He saw Mark making his way towards the monastery, and immediately dropped the cup on the ground and scurried downstairs as he loaded his pistol and switched off the safety lock. After the run-chase in Varanasi, they meet again now, in Gaya. As Ishir reached downstairs, he leaped towards a corner to find a place to hide. Ishir was planning an unexpected attack on Tanner while hiding.

Tanner reached the monastery's hall and saw that an elderly monk was walking outside the library. The monk was requested to leave, with protection, upon the request of the Remaining Four. He walked inside the hall where the Remaining Four and Ananya were standing. He pulled out his P92 pistol which contained a suppressor to suppress sound. He reloaded the pistol and pull the safety lock to turn it off and aimed at them, "You blokes are all dead now!" Ishir who was right behind him imitated Mark's British accent and said, "Not until you have fought me mate!" Mark turned around and saw Ishir who was pointing his pistol towards him and said, "Hello fellow mate! We meet again." Yet again mocking his British accent.

"Mark where are the previous nine manuscripts?" asked Ananya.

"With me. But they are going to be pretty useless considering that I'm going to take the manuscripts from Ashoka's Secret. But first, let me add a bullet to each of your bodies," answered Tanner as he switched off his pistol's safety lock and pointed his gun at Ishir.

Ananya came up with a quick change of plan and immediately ran towards the library of the monastery where Ashoka's Secret was supposed to be hidden. Once she reached the library with her bag, she saw one of Rinpoche's disciples who shuffled books in a certain manner and tilted Buddha's head to ninety degrees. The bookshelf slid horizontally and she saw a painting of the two Buddhist deities: Chakrasamvara and Vajrayogini. She removed the key from her bag and inserted it inside a keyhole on the bottom-left corner of the painting. The painting slid towards the left and there it was: Ashoka's Secret. A chest containing the nine manuscripts researched, updated, and protected by the Nine Unknown.

Ananya pulled out the chest from the shelf and placed it carefully on the ground. She settled down with one knee on the ground and saw the entire layout of the chest. In front of her was a screen, a keyboard with the keys in the Brahmi script, and a keyhole. On the top surface was the Ashokan symbol consisting of the four lions symbolising power, courage, confidence, and pride. The right surface consisted of the image of the Buddha and the left surface of the chest had the Buddhist lotus which holds a high significance in Buddhism.

Ananya removed the key from the painting of Chakrasamvara and Vajrayogini and inserted it inside the keyhole which activated a screen. When she noticed that the keyboard is in the Brahmi script, she pulled out a piece of paper which contained the Brahmi to English alphabet guide with the help of the Roman Harvard–Kyoto form of algorithm. The first question that popped up on the screen was: "I take refuge in the ..."

Ananya referred to her translation guide and connected the alphabets together with which she typed the word "Buddha" to complete the sentence "I take refuge in the Buddha". A second question popped up on the screen which again said "I take refuge in the..." Ananya looked for letters in Brahmi to form the word "Sangha" to complete the sentence "I take refuge in the Sangha." Another question popped up "I take refuge in the..." Ananya found letters on the Brahmi script to type the word "Dharma" to form the sentence "I take refuge in the Dharma" on the Brahmi keyboard of the chest.

Ananya expected that the chest could now be opened. But to her disappointment, there was another round of questions that came up on the screen. The first question was "A battlefield in present day Odisha is?" Ananya typed the word "Kalinga" on the keyboard. The second question popped up. Ananya was closer to opening the manuscripts and executing her plan. She could hear Ishir and Tanner fight with each other in the background. The second question was "The wheel of time is called?" Ananya typed "Kalachakra" on the keyboard and like that, another question popped up which said "The founder of the Nine Unknown Men is?" for which Ananya typed "Ashoka" on the Brahmi script keyboard. Finally, the chest slowly and automatically opened itself and she saw the nine manuscripts right in front of her eyes. She said to herself, "So it is true. The Nine Unknown actually do exist and so do their manuscripts." Ananya pulled the manuscripts out of the chest and closed the chest. She walked outside carrying the chest and a gun in her hand which had stolen from Ishir's car and kept in her bag. She walked towards the hall of the monastery. Ishir was fighting with Tanner and the Remaining Four were standing still, near the statue of the Buddha. They were waiting for Ananya's plan to execute.

Ananya announced, "Tanner, you want this chest right? Then here you go," Anaya tossed the chest in the air and suddenly time felt very slow for everyone who had their eyes aimed at the chest. Ananya immediately took the gun out and fired rounds at the chest. As soon as the chest slowly landed on the floor, it exploded in flames. Tanner shouted, "NOOOO!"

Ishir crouched towards his ankle, removed the revolver from his ankle holster and fired a few rounds at Mark Tanner. Mark Tanner collapsed on the ground after witnessing his plan failing and getting shot by someone who said that he will be Mark's biggest nightmare. Ishir opened Tanner's phone and entered the fingerprint with Tanner's thumb which opened the screen. Ishir opened the contact logs from his phone and saw the number of Richard Burton saved on his call logs. Ishir was shocked when he realised that a billionaire and philanthropist like Richard Burton is the mastermind behind this. Ishir dialled Burton's phone number, but Burton did not answer it. The Remaining Four and Ananya along with Ishir walked outside the monastery. Ananya noticed the ring on Ishir's ring finger and asked, "Does your wife know who you really are?"

Ishir replied, "She does not know who I am because she divorced me before I became a contract killer, a mercenary."

"How long has it been?" asked Ananya.

"Been quite a few years," answered Ishir.

"Yet, you still wear the ring. Doesn't time heal pain?" wondered Ananya.

"Time heals pain only when you are ready to accept it," said Ishir.

Tanner's phone rang. Ishir opened it and it was Richard Burton calling. Ishir answered the phone, and he heard a British accent with a deep voice that said, "Hey Tanner. You found the manuscripts?"

Ishir answered, "Tanner is useless, he is dead. I have the manuscripts with me. Tell me where to come, and I will bring them with me."

"How can I be so sure of you?" asked Burton.

"Is there anyone else who has the nine manuscripts? Or even knows about them?" asked Ishir rhetorically.

Burton smiled and said, "Come to a mansion called The Sword of Power in Hampshire, London."

Shilpa Dixit asked Ananya, "Ananya where are the manuscripts?"

Ananya smiled to that question in reply.

# CHAPTER 31

**London**
**United Kingdom**

Ishir was standing by the Westminster Bridge, waiting for his logistics supplier to contact and meet him. The locale around Westminster consisted of the famous Westminster bridge built above the Thames river and the British Parliament on his right with the Big Ben standing right next to the Parliament building. The three monuments were the architectural trinity of London and Westminster. Ishir was wearing his earphones to listen to the poem called "Westminster Bridge" written by William Wordsworth, which took him back in time to his childhood in Dehradun in a convent school. Happy memories of the past brought tears to his eyes as they were memories of innocence. Little did he know that the real world would be so harsh on him. Yet, he still had a job to do. And to save thousands of happy, innocent children, he had to kill, bleed, and dirty his hands.

Ishir received a call from a phone number saved as "Supplier". Ishir answered the call and the person on the other end said, "Meet me downstairs." Ishir walked to the staircase at the end of the Westminster bridge and trotted down the long staircase where he met his supplier who handed him a black-leathered duffel bag. The supplier said, "Received your payment, here are your tools."

"My car?" asked Ishir.

The supplier pointed to a black-coloured Mustang. Ishir turned around and caught a key tossed by his supplier mid-air and said, "What a beauty." Ishir walked towards the Mustang and tossed the duffel bag on the front seat. Ishir started the car and drove to Hampshire. Ishir wanted to eliminate the entirety of Sword of Power, especially liquidate the founder of that secret society: Richard Burton. After which, Ishir would go back to his next assignment. He understood that being the "Saviour of the Nine" would not be relevant anymore as the Nine Unknown and Ishir himself witnessed the effects of what happens when trust is betrayed. Ishir had to eliminate the Sword of Power now, and that is where his chapter with the Nine would end.

* * *

**Sword of Power Mansion**

**Hampshire**

**London**

Ishir's rented self-drive Mustang reached Hampshire to the Sword of Power mansion. Ishir called Burton from Tanner's phone. When Burton was present with all the members of the Sword of Power, he began the meeting. "Our objective has been achieved! Finally we can take control of the entire world. A man will be walking inside this secret society's safehouse and hand us over the nine manuscripts." Suddenly Burton received a call, "Yes Ishir. Have you reached?"

Ishir responded, "Mr. Burton, do you have any security?"

Burton replied, "None. Not even cameras. No digital footprint should capture any existence of us and nor should any security know about us. I have a button which will open the door for you. Should I open it now?"

"I will still take a while to reach. Once I reach, I will call you again." Saying this, Ishir disconnected the phone call. Ishir reached in a few minutes and to his surprise, he saw a few guards waiting outside the main gate of Richard's mansion. Ishir removed his pistol from the glove box. He rolled down the windows and the sunroof of his Mustang, stood on the car seat and began shooting the guards at the entrance. Ishir rammed his Mustang inside and ran over the iron barred gates to make his way inside the mansion. He removed his sub-machine gun and fired bullets at the remaining guards surrounding the premises. There were additional bodyguards inside the mansion carrying sub-machine guns. Ishir fired an entire magazine towards the commandos who were entering like termites through the mansion's main door. Ishir finished killing each of the commandos who were making their way out one after the other. The bodyguards who were flanking from the different ends of the mansion were gunned down.

When Ishir emptied his magazine, he tossed a grenade for the other commandos too.

The members of the Sword of Power were scared and threw their guns in self-defence, to protect themselves from Ishir when he comes. However, a few bodyguards armed with machine guns were inside the conference room of the Sword of Power to protect their boss Richard Burton and his friends. Ishir shot the window glass and tossed a tear gas grenade inside, which fell on the floor and exploded massive amounts of gas which made the members of the Sword of Power and their bodyguards step out of the room coughing. Ishir hopped inside the main door of the mansion and gunned down the bodyguards from the window who were protecting Richard Burton and his entourage.

He grabbed his duffel bag and walked inside the mansion's entrance. As Ishir made his way towards the entrance, he noticed a big wooden door with a golden lion's head which was the handle to open the door. After the tear gas settled in the room, the Sword of Power feared at their bodyguards being gunned down, and shifted inside the conference room again to seek shelter from Ishir.

Ishir walked inside the room which was a gigantic conference room. He looked at the people who were inside that room and called their names out, "Richard Burton, Yao Zhi, Kenny Roman, Lalit Bakshi, Dmitri Baladin, and Tobias Schneider," Ishir continued after a small pause, "The most popular scientists, businessmen, and media personalities are here. Little did the entire world know that all these famous bunch of people are a part of a blood-thirsty secret society which needs these nine manuscripts so that they can take control over the entire world. The purpose of the Nine Unknown was to preserve the nine manuscripts and reveal them only when the world is ready to accept change towards the progression of humanity."

"Your point?" asked Lalit Bakshi as he pointed the pistol towards Ishir.

Ishir slid down to the floor to quickly get out of the conference room. Yao Zhi, Kenny Roman, Dmitri Baladin, and Lalit Bakshi began firing rounds of bullets towards Ishir who was struggling to aim and shoot back at them. The bullet holes through the wooden doors could not protect Ishir anymore. He pulled out a grenade and walked inside the conference room. "I have the manuscripts and if you shoot me, then you won't know how to acccess them without me. Drop your weapons now, we can do this without violence as well."

The Sword of Power members dropped their weapons on the table. Kenny Roman asked, "Why did you start firing at us and our bodyguards?" Ishir pulled out his 9mm P92 Beretta and fired bullets starting with Kenny Roman, then Lalit Bakshi, after that at Yao Zhi and then shot a bullet towards the bald Russian scientist with light green eyes, Dmitri Baladin. Finally, he aimed at Richard Burton who pulled out his personal pistol which was aesthetically pleasing as it was plated in gold and silver. Ishir smirked, "Nice colour. Have you checked the safety lock?" Just as Burton was about to check the safety lock, Ishir pressed the trigger of the gun aimed at Burton's forehead. A perfect round bloodshot was created as the bullet hit his brain and Burton collapsed on the wooden floor with the chair falling on him.

Ishir unzipped the bag and planted dynamite explosives around the conference room of the Sword of Power. He switched on the detonator and sprinted outside the house reaching for the door of his Mustang. Ishir started the car and drove off from the Sword of Power mansion and about a few hundred meters later, Ishir pressed the trigger which led to a massive explosion, and the Sword of Power mansion burnt and collapsed in pieces along with the bodies of all members. Ishir called the RAW chief Suraj Khanna as he drove out of Hampshire and said—

"Mission accomplished, chief."

# CHAPTER 32

**9 years ago**
**10:00 a.m.**
**Piccadilly Circus**
**London**

Richard Burton invited Mark Tanner to an expensive restaurant in Central London. The media mogul spent his Sunday brunches at a restaurant right at the centre of the Piccadilly circus. This time, it was not just a casual Sunday brunch with any of his friends, eating a full English breakfast. He had invited an MI6 agent to join him for breakfast. The connection between Richard Burton and Mark Tanner was that Burton wanted some inside information about the MI6 and the previous government in exchange for money. Extortion was always the means for Burton to get any information possible. The shocking controversial facts and leaking of the scandalous lives of public figures is primarily what the News Bird's articles were flocking with. This time, the media giant had something in mutual favour for himself and the MI6 agent.

Exactly when Richard's watch showed 9:00 a.m., Mark entered the busy restaurant walking towards Richard's table wearing a beige formal jacket, brown pants, a cream-coloured shirt, and a light brown sweater over the shirt. He shook hands with Richard and greeted him using their mutual codename. "Good morning, Hercules."

Burton who was sipping onto his cup of tea put the cup down and shook hands with Mark using his codename. "Good morning, Orion." Burton took a pause for Tanner to sit on his chair, then began, "The reason why I called you is because I have something for you, an assignment which is double the price for something that is extremely valuable."

"But Richard, I am afraid that the department knows that I had leaked the information to someone. However, I have tried erasing whatever evidence that was possible from my end. But they have retrieved the pen drives which consists of all the surveillance data of whatever I have collected from my bank's locker. How do I get out of this chase?" Mark switched to using Richard's name rather than his codename. The codenames were used only during phone calls, emails, or messages. "Well...Mark," paused Richard as he too switched to first name basis rather than codenames. "I would like you to read this file. Richard opened his black leathered briefcase and fetched Mark a cardboard material file which was titled "The Nine Unknown", written in big capital letters using a red marker. Tanner opened the file and skimmed through each page that he turned. The documents in the file contained all the information that Richard's fact-checkers, researchers, journalists, assistants, and secretaries had verified about Ashoka and his secret society of the Nine Unknown. Tanner was surprised about an ancient Indian king's secret society preserving advanced knowledge. He believed that it was just some myth, folktale, or some conspiracy theory. However, Tanner took a moment to wonder why Richard Burton would be interested in this and why should he himself be involved in this.

"What do you expect me to do?" asked Tanner.

"I want you to take this file, read each and every word of it. Then do your own research about all the people who are big names in each of the nine subjects included in that file and bring their names to me," answered Burton.

"But why?" Tanner's questions kept flowing.

"This is to save you from the MI6. I am planning to start this secret society called the "Sword of Power" which will use the nine manuscripts for our benefit. Imagine, the knowledge that is being preserved by the Nine Unknown is so potent that it could change the world and he who holds it can basically play with the world on his fingertips," said Richard as he explained his plan to Tanner. He continued, "Since I know you won't tell this to anyone and agents from the MI6 are on the chase, they are monitoring you at every step of the way, I have an offer for you: come work for me for triple the price once you kill all the Nine Unknown and get those manuscripts for me. In exchange, I will make some contact with the government and the MI6 agents related to exposing them and their double-lives to the public."

Tanner agreed but he had another question, "I am totally flattered by this plan Richie, believe me I really am. But what if this entire matter about you exposing them is taken to court? What if there is some other action that is taken against you?"

"If Richard Burton, the greatest media mogul, more or less the media mafia, can have secrets about the Royal Family. Then it is easy for me to find any dirt on anyone. My contacts are so strong that even my own ex-wife couldn't expose me, in spite of me having multiple affairs as a married man. She just took the money and fled the country. I have done the same thing to all of my girlfriends," said Burton arrogantly as he spoke of his frivolous relationships which were filled with infidelity.

"So what am I supposed to do?" Tanner asked his final question as he bit his tongue to the realisation about asking to many questions and irritating the powerful media mogul.

"You are supposed to read that file, find me professionals for each of the nine fields and I want to know their entire background filled with each and every detail. You might as well put in their favourite ice-cream flavour if you'd like," joked Burton as he continued. "Also, don't forget to mention the football teams they support." The two gentlemen exchanged laughter over their full-English breakfast. "But jokes apart, after you bring their file to me. I want you to go into your own research and find the Nine Unknown. Once you do that, you have to become a part of the Nine Unknown as their "Saviour or Guardian". Then we will plot out the perfect plan to hunt them down and snatch their control over those manuscripts and nothing could stop us!' said Burton as his voice went deeper and his pitch went a little higher.

* * *

**Richard Burton's Mansion**
**Hampshire**
**London**

Mark Tanner had read the file that Burton had given. He took a week to research completely about the king Ashoka and his secret society: The Nine Unknown. Mark also came across a book that had been written by a British army officer who had discovered this secret society and decided to write a fictional novel about it. However, that could not be considered as history. The novel has several rumours about how the British officer had come across nine such manuscripts of Ashoka about the nine diverse subjects written in the Brahmi, Pali, and Prakrit scripts during the course of his research, which actually led him to writing a novel about the secret society.

A week after compiling all the research required in a binder, Mark drove his car towards Hampshire where Burton lived. As he drove down the neighbourhood, he came across this isolated mansion which was on the outskirts of

Hampshire. The mansion was secured and guarded with muscular bodyguards. He parked his car outside the mansion; however, the cameras beamed a laser scan over the car's number plate and over the driver. The doors automatically opened and Tanner reluctantly drove inside the mansion. He said to himself as he drove a few meters inside the entire estate of the mansion and the lush green lawns next to which were stables consisting of stallions, "Bloody hell! Mate lives like Bruce Wayne." Mark was referencing Batman as he drove inside. A bodyguard stopped Mark and asked him to step out of the car. The muscular guard had tattoos on his arm wearing shades and a black pistol holstered around the shoulder.

Another guard escorted Tanner from the car to the mansion as he spoke on his earpiece, "Yes Hercules, I have Orion, he is on his way to the Cave." The guards too spoke in coded language as instructed by Burton who made an entire list of codenames. Tanner who was holding the binder in his hand had a gun that was on his ankle holster. Before the guards on the door's entrance could open the door for him, Tanner had to walk through a scanner which detected a gun and alarmed the guards. Tanner reached for his gun and threw it on the ground.

Finally, Mark walked inside the mansion. The guard pressed the biometric scanner which opened the door automatically to a ballroom leading to a huge conference room table where Burton was seated. Mark walked towards the chair next to it and sat down, keeping the binder on the table. Burton who was enjoying a cigar greeted him, "Well, hello Mark! Looks like you did your homework eh. Fancy a cigar or a drink if you'd like."

Mark reluctantly picked the cigar from the box of the expensive Cuban collection and slowly yet hesitantly poured the expensive liquor in a glass. Burton began, "Let's get to work. What have you found?"

Tanner said, "Everything that is related to Ashoka and the Nine Unknown is in this binder." Tanner pushed the binder to Burton which shook the glass of Burton's liquor, but Burton's reflexes saved the glass from falling. "Get to the point. Did you find me the members of the Sword of Power?" Burton asked.

"Yes," He pulled out a few papers from the binder which consisted of the detailed information regarding each potential candidate who would be a member of the Sword of Power. "This list includes scientists like Yao Zhi, Dmitri Baladin, Tobias Schneider, and Lalit Bakshi."

"Alright. Now it is my job to get them on board," said Burton as he took a puff of his cigar. "Your job is to find a way to get in contact with the Nine Unknown. Now tell me how do you plan to do that?" asked Richard who started mildly coughing after smoking his cigar.

"There is an unknown library in Dharamshala which stores all the works of the Nine Unknown and only the Nine Unknown have access to it. The library has never been opened and according to what my sources tell me, there is a speculative address of the library which states that it is located in a Buddhist monastery on the hills of Karnataka," said Tanner.

"What is the plan?" emphasised Richard.

"I will book a flight to Bangalore. There is a key in a cave in Kanakpura which is about three hours away from Bangalore. Once I find the key over there, I will open the library in Dharamshala," answered Tanner.

# CHAPTER 33

**9 years ago**
**Kanakpura**
**Karnataka**
**India**

Mark arrived in Bangalore and drove from the Bangalore airport to Kanakpura which was a village surrounded by lush greenery, heavy boulders, and hills. According to Tanner's sources, the address mentioned on the locked, hidden library's board in Dharamshala led to a cave in Kanakpura. Tanner referred to all the GPS systems to locate the actual location. All of which showed an unexplored cave in Kanakpura. And here was Tanner who trekked all over the hills of Karnataka's Kanakpura for nine hours to eventually find the cave.

He climbed over and around the boulders and trekked over six different terrains to find this hidden cave and now here he was. But the mission for Tanner was just not over yet. Mark sneaked inside the cave which was one directional and narrow. He felt short of breath and claustrophobic but he continued to the point where the cave ended. He looked around the cave, he saw the inscriptions carved on the walls of the cave, and these inscriptions were symbols of languages that he could not understand. However, he could see the tracings of a certain type of a key in front of him. He removed his Swiss army knife out of his bag and scraped traced lines on the wall. Once the tracing was scraped using his knife, he pushed it with hands which fell out on itself and found himself a radiant, golden, and brightly shining key. Once Tanner got out of the cave and found his car, he was on his way to Dharamshala.

* * *

**Dharamshala**
**Himachal Pradesh**

After a tiring hunt for the key in Kanakpura, Mark had finally reached Dharamshala where the library was located. The library was on the outskirts of a remote village in Dharamshala. The city Dharamshala was home to the Buddhist community and exclusively Rinpoche who resided in McLeod Ganj where the government gave him the authority to run his government-in-exile. Since there are a lot of Tibetans from Lhasa who escaped the Chinese occupied Tibet under Mao Zedong's rule and took refuge in Dharamshala, because of that Dharamshala is also called "Little Lhasa".

Mark drove his jeep in the icy and snowy hilly areas of the remote village just outside of Dharamshala. There was no network for Mark to locate this library, he was compelled to ask someone about it. In his broken Hindi, he asked one of the villagers about the library. The villagers gathered to see a foreigner inside a remote village. They all assumed that he was just some tourist who lost his way, but when he talked about the library, there was suspicion amongst the villagers. A couple of villagers directed him to the library and as they walked, someone used a club to knock down Tanner's head to make him unconscious.

* * *

**A few days later**

Mark Tanner woke up in a small house of the village, noticing the snowfall outside, he assumed that he was still in Dharamshala. As he woke up, he saw an old woman in her seventies holding a walking stick sitting on a chair saying, "Mark Tanner, why the hell were you asking about this library?"

The lady's attire was much different that the local villagers, her features were also quite different from the local villagers and even her accent was different as compared to the dialects and accents that he grasped from communicating with the villagers. He asked, "Who are you? A member of the Nine Unknown?"

The woman was Nivedita Kaur, head of the Nine Unknown. "It is quite rare that someone actually inquires, let alone walks inside the library you were looking for. I got this key in your pocket." Nivedita Kaur showed the golden key to Tanner. "I am here because I wanted to establish contact with the Nine Unknown," replied Tanner.

"Why so?" asked Kaur.

"Because I have reason to believe that the Nine Unknown is in possible danger and I want to offer my role as the Saviour of the Nine Unknown. I will guard you from all threats and I will arrange all the logistics from my end," answered Tanner.

"But why should you work for the Nine Unknown?" asked Kaur.

"I was an MI6 agent, and I know that governments and well-renowned businessmen are coming together to hunt you down as their pet project. My own research tells me that even the Chinese have access to this information. And if I, an individual could find a key from an unknown cave in Kanakpura then imagine the kind of resources that the government could use at their disposal. I know how these governments think and the MI6 is on the hunt for me because I know their dirty little secrets. How they guard it, how they create it, and how do they bury it. If I can think two steps ahead of these people then I can also predict the next secret that they are going to create and cover up, including the fact that they are on the hunt for you guys. Let me help you and guard you. I promise that you won't die in their hands," explained Tanner as he came up with a lie to justify himself in order to work for the Nine Unknown. Soon enough, Mark Tanner had become the Saviour of the Nine.

# Part Three

# 4 YEARS LATER
# PRESENT DAY

# CHAPTER 34

**6:00 p.m.**
**Delhi**
**India**

Years after Ananya completed her graduation, she landed a job as a content writer for a media company's history department. She was living in an apartment in Delhi with a friend from college. It had been four years after she had been a part of an adventure with the Nine Unknown, an adventure that also consisted of a lot of violence and blood being shed. After the explosion of Ashoka's Secret, Ananya handed over nine books from her bag and immediately left for Delhi and started trying to forget what had happened.

Years after that incident, Ananya was now about to complete her PhD thesis and was planning for PhD defences going forward for her research paper. After her guide's death, she decided to not take her PhD research anywhere near any secret society or the Nine Unknown. In spite of conducting an abundant amount of research on Ashoka, secret societies, the Nine Unknown, and sociology, she felt dejected when she had to change her subject for her PhD research. However, her passion for history laid somewhere in Ancient India and Archeology, and she was eager to pursue it. She diverted her research from secret societies and sociology and directed her research towards Ancient India.

As Ananya was working in her bedroom's study table on the weekend on an assignment, suddenly her doorbell rang. She walked from her bedroom towards the door assuming that it would be her roommate waiting outside the door, but as she opened the door, she saw Dr. Leena Gokhale, the head of the Nine Unknown. Dr. Gokhale said, "Something important."

Ananya welcomed her inside her apartment and offered her a glass of water. As Ananya asked to offer tea and biscuits, Dr. Gokhale declined and said that she needs to talk to her inside her room so that no one is able to hear her. Gokhale rested on Ananya's chair while Ananya sat on the study table. Her table lamp's light was shining bright on her desk. Gokhale began, "We have recruited a new batch of the Nine Unknown and the manuscripts are safe. After what happened four years ago, we may have been compromised so we have decided to go on radio silence and cut all ties with everyone we were connected with. Now we are underground."

Ananya asked, "Why are you telling me all of this? Why am I being a part of this treasure hunt that Mark Tanner started?"

Gokhale smiled and replied, "Because we were wondering if you could be a possible replacement for the guardian of Sociology. You would be replacing Nivedita Kaur and would be researching, updating, and also safeguarding the Manuscript of Sociology. What say?"

Ananya took a few seconds to pause. She was shocked by what Gokhale had offered, she said "I am a little shocked. My present research is directed towards history. All research I conducted about Sociology previously is of no use to me, but I did not realise I could be doing something related to Sociology as my passion lies towards history."

"So did Nivedita. She wanted to be a professor of Ancient Indian studies yet she had to master the subject of Sociology because that is what she had been assigned to do," said Dr. Gokhale as she remembered her friend and colleague.

"What was the purpose of doing it for so long? Why did the Sword of Power and Mark Tanner chase you guys?" asked Ananya as she wanted to digress from the question.

"Because there is a fine line between curiosity and greed for knowledge. Curiosity for knowledge is when us, the Nine Unknown want to research more about things for the improvement of the world. People like Richard Burton and his Sword of Power were greedy for knowledge because all they wanted was to get their hands on these nine manuscripts, so that they could control this entire world," explained Dr. Gokhale.

Ananya remembered, "You mentioned that there are Ashoka's three keys. One is with the head of the Nine, second one is found with the help of a map. What about the third one?"

Dr. Gokhale had a mysterious smile, her green eyes stared at Ananya. She said, "You are a good human being and a good student. You graduated as a double major student that too with perfect scores, and were an integral part of the highly sensitive mission of the Nine Unknown a few years ago. Only because you love research and have the desire to learn and excel. So, if you want to know more about Ashoka's third key and continue your professor's legacy..."

Ananya took a moment to think. She wanted to be an archaeologist and sociology was something she was good at but did not feel like pursuing it. Her love for the subject of India's history was linked to Archaeology. Now she had the moment to decide. Everything blurred for Ananya.

Gokhale finally asked, "Ananya Kulkarni, will you join the Nine Unknown?"

# CHARACTER LIST

**Ananya Kulkarni:** Main protagonist, student of Nivedita Kaur and a PhD student researching on the connections of secret societies with sociology.

**Ishir Singh:** Former Major of the Paramilitary, Commander of the mercenary group 'The Wolf's Claw'.

**Mark Tanner:** Ex-MI6 agent and henchman of the Sword of Power.

**Paula Maxwell:** Microbiologist and member of the Nine Unknown.

**Shilpa Dixit:** Space scientist, researcher on Cosmology, and member of the Nine Unknown.

**Leena Gokhale:** Microbiologist, second-in-command, and member of the Nine Unknown

**Nivedita Kaur:** Ananya's PhD guide, Professor of Sociology, and the head of the Nine Unknown.

**Stefan Schmidt:** Light engineer and member of the Nine Unknown.

**Isaac Joseph:** Astrophysicist, researcher on Gravity, and member of the Nine Unknown.

**Rupert Roy:** Veteran journalist, researcher on propaganda, and member of the Nine Unknown.

**Ashwin Tripathi:** Physiologist, surgeon, and member of the Nine Unknown.

**Richard Burton:** Media mogul, business tycoon, and head of the Sword of Power.

**Kenny Roman:** Media entrepreneur, journalist, and member of the Sword of Power.

**Yao Zhi:** Chinese light engineer and member of the Sword of Power.

**Cheng Zhang:** Former Chinese MSS agent.

**Lalit Bakshi:** Indian scientist and member of the Sword of Power.

**Dmitri Baladin:** Former Russian space scientist of the Roscosmos and member of the Sword of Power.

**Tobias Schneider:** German physicist and member of the Sword of Power.

**Tenzing Rinpoche:** A Tibetan monk affiliated with the Nine Unknown.

**Eric Silva:** Logistician of the Sword of Power.

**Ashoka:** Former king of the Mauryan dynasty and founder of the secret society called the Nine Unknown.

**Samudra:** Ashoka's guru and supposedly the reincarnation of Padmasambhava.

**Upadatta:** Ashoka's mentor.

# CITATIONS

*Buy The Nine Unknown Book Online at Low Prices in India | The Nine Unknown Reviews & Ratings - Amazon.in.* (2019, January 13). Buy the Nine Unknown Book Online at Low Prices in India | the Nine Unknown Reviews & Ratings - Amazon.in. https://www.amazon.in/Nine-Talbot-Mundy/dp/1515439984/ref=sr_1_2?crid=FQDQUR22S3RA&keywords=the+nine+unknown&qid=1648053522&sprefix=the+nine+unknow%2Caps%2C280&sr=8-2

*Ashok and the Nine Unknown : Anshul Dupare: Amazon.in: Books.* (2018, November 20). Ashok and the Nine Unknown : Anshul Dupare: Amazon.in: Books. https://www.amazon.in/Ashok-Nine-Anshul-Dupare/dp/9353047641/ref=sr_1_1?crid=FQDQUR22S3RA&keywords=the+nine+unknown&qid=1648053522&sprefix=the+nine+unknow%2Caps%2C280&sr=8-1

*Buy The Nine Unknown (Mint Editions) Book Online at Low Prices in India | The Nine Unknown (Mint Editions)*

*Reviews & Ratings - Amazon.in.* (2021, August 10). Buy the Nine Unknown (Mint Editions) Book Online at Low Prices in India | the Nine Unknown (Mint Editions) Reviews & Ratings - Amazon.in. https://www.amazon.in/Nine-Mint-Editions-Talbot-Mundy/dp/1513206079/ref=sr_1_3?crid=FQDQUR22S3RA&keywords=the+nine+unknown&qid=1648053522&sprefix=the+nine+unknow%2Caps%2C280&sr=8-3

*The mystery of 9 Unknown Men | Indian Illuminati | Emperor Ashoka | Nutshell.* (2021, July 23). YouTube. https://www.youtube.com/watch?v=fdypA_BxYa0

*9 Mystery Men of Ashoka | Ancient Indian illuminati | RAAAZ Hindi Video ft. @Amanjain0907.* (2022, January 5). YouTube. https://www.youtube.com/watch?v=x2L-jNuLCY4

*9 Mystery Men of Ashoka | Ancient Indian illuminati | RAAAZ Hindi Video ft. @Amanjain0907.* (2022, January 5). YouTube. https://www.youtube.com/watch?v=x2L-jNuLCY4

B. (n.d.). *British Architectural Styles.* British Architectural Styles. https://www.bohaglass.co.uk/british-architectural-styles/

*Fergusson College, Pune.* (n.d.). Fergusson College, Pune. https://www.fergusson.edu/

*All About Ashoka's 9 Unknown Men, A 2000-YO Secret Society That Perhaps Exists Even Today.* (2021, June 30). www.mensxp.com. https://www.mensxp.com/culture/people/89892-9-unknown-men-ashoka-secret-society-india-illuminati.html

*Kalinga War | Mauryan Empire [UPSC History Notes].* (n.d.). BYJUS. https://byjus.com/free-ias-prep/kalinga-war/

*Ashoka's Conversion | World Civilization.* (n.d.). Ashoka's Conversion | World Civilization. https://courses.lumenlearning.com/suny-hccc-worldcivilization/chapter/ashokas-conversion/

*Lomas Rishi Cave - Wikipedia.* (2015, January 8). Lomas Rishi Cave - Wikipedia. https://en.wikipedia.org/wiki/Lomas_Rishi_Cave

*Lomas Rishi Cave, Barabar Hills, Gaya, Bihar.* (2019, August 10). Rana Safvi. https://ranasafvi.com/lomas-rishi-cave-barabar-hills-gaya-bihar/

*Excavations in Mauryan Site.* (n.d.). IndiaNetzone.com. https://www.indianetzone.com/70/relics_kumhrar.htm

Mark, J. J. (n.d.). *Ashoka the Great.* World History Encyclopedia. https://www.worldhistory.org/Ashoka_the_Great /

*Mauryan Empire.* (n.d.). Mauryan Empire. https://education.nationalgeographic.org/resource/mauryan-empire

*Ashoka's 9 Unknown Men (Secret Society): Real Or Myth? | #AskAbhijit E10Q9 | Abhijit Chavda.* (2021, July 15). YouTube. https://www.youtube.com/watch?v=kmgTCI_bzOU

*The Ancient SECRET Society of The NINE Unknown Men.* (2017, September 22). YouTube. https://www.youtube.com/watch?v=0gW9m5_7avg

*Ashoka the Great - Rise of the Mauryan Empire Documentary.* (2019, April 18). YouTube. https://www.youtube.com/watch?v=Ed6UZtVTI64

*Bharatvarsh: Episode 3: Story of Mauryan emperor Ashoka Samrat.* (2016, September 5). YouTube. https://www.youtube.com/watch?v=ChS9GVbCUjA

*Why Emperor Ashoka wanted Kalinga | Stories that Make India.* (2022, September 24). YouTube. https://www.youtube.com/watch?v=eUCBoUd5EJ0

*Alchemy - Transmuting, Prolonging Life, and Hermetic Literature.* (n.d.). Encyclopedia Britannica. https://www.britannica.com/topic/alchemy

Kharakwal, J. S., & Gurjar, L. K. (2006, December 1). *Zinc and Brass in Archaeological Perspective.* Zinc and Brass in Archaeological Perspective - Ancient Asia. https://doi.org/10.5334/aa.06112

*Gravitation.* (n.d.). Gravitation. https://www.cs.mcgill.ca/~rwest/wikispeedia/wpcd/wp/g/Gravitation.html

*Light | Definition, Properties, Physics, Characteristics, Types, & Facts.* (n.d.). Encyclopedia Britannica. https://www.britannica.com/science/light

Project, T. N. (2020, May 19). *The meaning of Om Mani Padme Hum.* Tibetan Nuns Project. https://tnp.org/the-meaning-of-om-mani-padme-hum/

*Unlocking the Secrets of Om Mani Padme Hum | Ringu Tulku.* (2023, May 10). YouTube. https://www.youtube.com/watch?v=Y0u95-ITsIQ

*The Expansion of Buddhism.* (n.d.). The Expansion of Buddhism | the Pluralism Project. https://pluralism.org/the-expansion-of-buddhism#:~:text=As%20early%20as%20the%203rd,are%20now%20Myanmar%20and%20Thailand.

*The Legend of King Aśoka.* (n.d.). Google Books. https://books.google.com/books/about/The_Legend_of_King_A%C5%9Boka.html?id=Kp9uaQTQ8h8C

*Padmasambhava | Buddhist mystic.* (n.d.). Encyclopedia Britannica. https://www.britannica.com/biography/Padmasambhava

*Who is Padmasambhava? – Padmasambhava Buddhist Center.* (n.d.). Who Is Padmasambhava? – Padmasambhava Buddhist Center. https://www.padmasambhava.org/who-is-padmasambhava/

*Delhi's Ashoka Connection.* (2018, July 12). PeepulTree. https://www.peepultree.world/livehistoryindia/story/places/delhis-ashoka-connects

*Feroz Shah Kotla Fort | Incredible India.* (n.d.). Feroz Shah Kotla Fort | Incredible India. https://www.incredibleindia.org/content/incredible-india-v2/en/destinations/delhi/feroz-shah-kotla-fort.html

*Topra Ashokan pillar, Feroz Shah Kotla, Dehli, India, 1965-2000.* (n.d.). CONTENTdm. https://digitalcollections.lib.washington.edu/digital/collection/ic/id/10600/

*Brass Blessing - ASHOK STAMBH ROUND PLAT ( 9") ENGRAVING. . .* (n.d.). https://m.facebook.com/brassblessing/photos/ashok-stambh-round-plat-9engraving-ashok-stambh-material-brassweight-037-kg-size/2935462966472958/

*File:Barabar caves map.jpg - Wikimedia Commons.* (1871, January 1). https://commons.wikimedia.org/wiki/File:Barabar_caves_map.jpg

*Map | Welcome to UP Tourism-Official Website of Department of Tourism, Government of Uttar Pradesh, India.* (n.d.). https://www.uptourism.gov.in/en/page/map

*Firoz Shah Kotla - Google Arts & Culture.* (n.d.). Google Arts & Culture. https://artsandculture.google.com/story/IQVRRevlyR4A8A

*Experience | Heritage | Dhamek Stupa | Welcome to UP Tourism-Official Website of Department of Tourism, Government of Uttar Pradesh, India.* (n.d.). Experience | Heritage | Dhamek Stupa | Welcome to UP Tourism-Official Website of Department of Tourism, Government of Uttar Pradesh, India. https://www.uptourism.gov.in/en/page/dhamek-stupa#:~:text=Dhamek%20Stupa%20is%20the%20most,the%20deer%20park%20(Rishipattana).

The Life and Career of Major Jonathan Duncan 1756-1795: A thesis submitted by VA Narain to the University of London for the degree of Doctor of Philosophy (PhD) in June 1958

*Sarnath: Where Buddha Spoke.* (2020, May 4). PeepulTree. https://www.peepultree.world/livehistoryindia/story/monuments/sarnath

Singh, A. (2023, May 29). *Sarnath Pillar Stupa Museum and Tourism Information.* Varanasi.org.in. https://www.varanasi.org.in/sarnath

*The lost Sanskrit treasures of Tibet.* (2017, June 12). India Today. https://www.indiatoday.in/magazine/neighbours/story/20170612-sanskrit-tibet-chinese-scholars-buddhism-986510-2017-06-03

*The British Library Kharoṣṭhī Fragments | Asian Languages & Literature | University of Washington.* (n.d.). The British Library Kharoṣṭhī Fragments | Asian Languages & Literature | University of Washington. https://asian.washington.edu/british-library-kharosthi-fragments

The Tibetan Dunhuang Manuscripts in China | Sam Van Schnaik | Bulletin of the School of Oriental and African Studies, University of London | Published by Cambridge University Press. https://www.jstor.org/stable/414590446.

Sarkar, M. (2023, October 16). *The Nine Unknown Men: Great Ashoka's Secret Society.* Unrevealed Files. https://www.unrevealedfiles.com/the-nine-unknown-great-ashokas-secret-society/47. Patgaonkar, J. (2022, January 21). *Library of Tibetan Works and Archives: Surviving Against All Odds.* PeepulTree. https://www.peepultree.world/livehistoryindia/story/heritage-matters/library-of-tibetan-works-and-archives

# ABOUT THE AUTHOR

**Chinmay Patgaonkar** is a teenager studying at Indus International School Pune. He loves writing, reading, and traveling to new places. He takes a fervid interest in history, movies, books, and sports. Above all, he loves meeting people and exchanging stories.

He published his first novel in 2022 titled *The Last 21 Hours: A Bullet That Shook the White House.* Amid his rigorous IBDP academics, Chinmay finds time to dive into his fictional world and create stories. He lives in Pune with his parents, grandparents, his sister, and his dog Angel.